An Augathella Masquerade Ball

ANNIE SEATON

Augathella Short and Sweet: 7

AUGATHELLA SHORT AND SWEETS
An Augathella Surprise
An Augathella Baby
An Augathella Spring
An Augathella Christmas
An Augathella Wedding
An Augathella Easter
An Augathella Masquerade Ball

Following on from:
THE AUGATHELLA GIRLS
Book 1: Outback Roads –The Nanny
Book 2: Outback Sky – The Pilot
Book 3: Outback Escape – The Sister
Book 4: Outback Winds – The Jillaroo
Book 5: Outback Dawn – The Visitor
Book 6: Outback Moonlight – The Rogue
Book 7: Outback Dust – The Drifter
Book 8: Outback Hope – The Farmer

CHAPTER 1
The Cartwrights - Kilcoy Station

Braden Cartwright rolled over, forced one eyelid open and groaned when the red numbers displayed on the bedside clock radio showed it was well past time he should be out of bed. With both eyes still closed, he reached over to cuddle Callie, but her side of the bed was cold and empty. He rolled onto his back and slowly forced both eyes open. The twins had both woken up at three o'clock, and he'd managed to get to the nursery next to the master bedroom before they'd disturbed Callie.

Callie needed her sleep; she'd had a head cold all week and had insisted last night that she was well enough to go back to work today. 'I've got some special sports thing on today. I promised my class it would be today, and they're so looking forward to it,' she said. 'Plus, there's a masquerade ball organising meeting straight after school, and I've somehow ended up as president.'

Braden had quirked an eyebrow. 'Somehow?'

'Well . . .'

'It's just that you love to help wherever you can. No wonder you're tired and picking up everything the kids bring home from school.'

Callie had smiled. 'Bring home? I'm there too.'

'I know. But you can't go in with a cold,' he said.

'It's almost gone. My throat's not sore anymore. I haven't got a headache, and my head's pretty clear. I'll just dose up on some antihistamines to stop my nose running all day. And don't worry, I've done two COVID tests, and they were negative. I think the twins have passed the bug on to me after they caught it off Ryan Ingram at Ruth's last week.'

'Well, as long as you feel well enough in the morning,' Braden said when they went to bed. 'You know you can't overdo it. Not only with the boys and the twins to look after, you have to think about the baby on the way, too.'

'And about you too, my sweet,' she said, patting his cheek.

'A tough cattleman doesn't need looking after,' he teased her.

Callie didn't reply. She was asleep as soon as her head hit the pillow.

So, when Braden heard the twins stirring in the early hours, he quickly got out of bed and closed the door. Megan and Munro were both teething, and all they wanted was a bit of a cuddle. He changed their nappies and rocked them both back to sleep, managing not to have to do the whole bottle thing.

When Callie got up, he must have been out like a light. A glimmer of light shone from the kitchen end of the hallway as he climbed out of bed, pulled on his jeans and flannelette shirt, and then padded barefoot to the kitchen.

On his way past, Braden glanced into the nursery and was pleased to see that everything was quiet; two little mounds were still under the blankets in both cots. Nigel and Petie were still sound asleep in their room, but Rory's bed was neatly made. As Braden approached the kitchen, his eldest son's voice reached him.

'He's a cool kid, Mum.'

'I don't know him,' Callie said. 'When did he start at the school?'

'When you were home sick,' Rory said, smiling when he saw Braden come in the door. 'Morning, Dad.' He turned back to Callie. 'He's a really good footballer. I reckon he'll play for the NRL one day.'

Braden went over to the coffee machine and switched it on. 'Who are we talking about?' he asked, rubbing his hand over his face. He'd forgo a shave this morning since he'd slept in.

'Sit down, Braden, and try to wake up. I'll make your coffee for you.' Callie came over as soon as he sat at the table and dropped a kiss on the top of his head. 'Thanks for getting up and seeing to the twins. I thought you'd sleep a bit longer.'

Braden wasn't a morning person, which wasn't a good thing for a cattleman, but he would be okay as soon as he had his coffee hit. 'What are *you* doing up so early?' he said.

'Well, I'm feeling much better thanks to an unbroken night's sleep, so I'm going to school, okay?'

Callie did look better than she had last night. She crossed to the coffee machine.

'I've got a lot to prepare for my class this morning, so I want to get into town early. I texted Ruth last night on the off chance that I'd be going in, and she said it's fine to bring the twins in as early as I want to. Rory, you three boys will have to sit in the staffroom for the first half hour when we get to school.'

Braden shook his head. 'It's okay, Cal. I have to go into town and meet Jon Ingram at the rural store this morning. He's dropping Ryan at Ruth's because Fallon is mustering today. She has to drive to Charleville for the helicopter. I'll run the boys in.'

'That'd be a great help. Thank you, sweetheart.'

'So, what's the plan? Lamb shanks for dinner?' He spotted them thawing out on the sink.

'Yep, I'll put them in the slow cooker before we go. Rory, there's a load of towels in the machine. While I have my shower, can you peg them on the line in the breezeway for me, love? And then get them in this afternoon? I've got a ball meeting after school.'

'Yes, Mum. But you haven't answered my question…'

'Sorry, I got sidetracked.' Callie reached up and pushed her hair back as she stirred the porridge. 'Tell me more about this new friend.'

'He came to school last week, and we're good mates already. I said he might be able to come out and play footy after school this afternoon. He could come home on the bus with me unless you're picking us up, Dad.' Rory turned to Braden with a hopeful look.

'Yes, I am, but remember, we're a long way out. If he comes here, we've got to run him back into town unless his parents pick him up. Who are they? Where do they live?'

'He hasn't got a mum. He said his carer would be happy to come out here and pick him up,' Rory said as he put a bit of bread in the toaster. 'Do you want some toast, Dad?'

'Thanks, mate, that would be great.'

'Who's having porridge?' Callie asked.

'I will,' Braden said. 'I'll start with toast with my coffee.'

'So, keep going,' Callie continued. 'What's his name? Whose class is he in?'

'His name is Beau, and he's in Mr Cooper's class. He's had a couple of days off since he started at school because his carer makes him work around the house,' Rory said.

Braden and Callie's eyes met over the top of Rory's head. Rory tended to pick up the needy kids at school, and Callie kept a close eye on him. He'd been burned a couple of times. The last time they'd discovered he'd been buying lunch at the canteen for a student who hid his lunch so Rory would buy him a pie. It happened every day for a week until Ros at the canteen told Callie what was going on. The only day the boys bought their lunch at the canteen was Monday, so Rory took money out of his money box and bought lunch for someone he thought was a needy student.

'It's not going to be Lucas Jones all over again, is it?' Callie asked.

'No, Mum. Beau's a really good guy, and like I said, he plays football, and we hit it off like a house on fire.'

Braden smothered a smile. 'Well, Mum can suss it out today and find out what the story is with getting picked up. Maybe Beau can come out on the weekend,' he said. 'Today's a bit short notice to organise him getting home.'

'Okay, I guess that's alright. I'll go and hang that washing out now. Here's your toast, Dad.' Rory laughed as Braden lifted his hands just in time to catch the piece of toast Rory frisbeed across from the toaster.

'Good catch, Dad.'

'Eat your porridge before you hang the washing, mate,' Callie said.

'Aw, Mum. You know I hate that gluggy stuff.'

'It's good for you.'

'I like porridge,' Nigel muttered as he came into the kitchen and sat at the table.

Callie grinned as she poured Braden's coffee. Nigel took after his father; he was not a morning person. Sometimes, he managed to eat his entire bowl of porridge without opening his eyes.

'Okay, I'll go and get ready. Now,' she said as she put the mug of coffee in front of Braden. 'Rory, don't forget the towels. And Nigel, you can feed the dogs for Dad this morning.'

'What about Petie? What's his job?' Nigel muttered crossly. 'I wish I was the baby of the family.'

'Petie's not the baby anymore, dumb-arse.'

Callie drew in a breath. 'Rory Cartwright, I beg your pardon. What did you say?'

Braden reached out and pulled Rory over to him. 'That's not a word we use in this house, Rory.'

'It's just a word,' Rory said defiantly. 'Just a mix of letters.'

'It's rude, and it wasn't good to call me that.'

Nigel was wide awake now.

'I'm sorry. I take it back,' Rory mumbled.

'Good, now eat your porridge and then go and hang those towels out for Mum.' Braden caught Callie's hand as she hurried past. 'Slow down. Are you sure you're well enough to go to school?'

'I am.' She smiled at him. 'I'm going for a shower. Cross your fingers that the twins sleep a little bit longer.'

CHAPTER 2

Getting six-year-old Petie out of bed on cold winter mornings was a chore in itself. By the time Braden had the three boys ready to go to school, their lunches packed, the dogs fed, and the twin cab ute backed out of the shed, they were running late. He tore off down the dirt road and was pulled up by his youngest son within seconds.

'Dad, you're going too fast. Mum said you always drive too fast, and she's not here, so I'm telling you to slow down. Got it?'

Braden bit back a grin and nodded. 'Sorry, Petie. I *was* going a little bit too fast. I'll slow down. If you're late for school, you're late for school. So be it.'

That started a fight between Rory and Nigel in the back seat. 'If we're late, I'm taking the football back into the sports storeroom when the bell goes,' Rory said.

Nigel shook his head, and Braden heard a thump from the backseat.

'No, you're not. It's my turn to do that.' Nigel was building up to a whine.

Braden threw a glance over his shoulder. 'If we're late, we'll miss the bell, and I'm sure the football will be put away by then anyway. Besides, that's not a thing to fight about, okay?'

All was quiet for about ten minutes, and then Rory leaned forward and put his hands on Braden's shoulders from the backseat.

'Dad?' he said.

Braden waited. By the tone of his voice and the soft touch of his eldest son's hands on his shoulders, he knew a favour was about to be asked. 'Yeah, mate, what's up?'

'I was really hoping Beau could come out and play football with me this afternoon. What do you think about that? Mum will be at her meeting, and the dinner's cooked, and he can help me with the chores before we play footy.'

'Can I play footy too?' Petie asked.

'No, Beau's my friend, and you're still too little. We can't tackle you,' Rory said.

Petie grunted.

'What's Beau's last name?' Braden asked. 'Does he live in town or on a property? Depends where he has to go home to.'

'I don't know his last name. I never took much notice. I only hear the first name in class when they mark the roll.'

'Well, I don't know if I know his family.'

'You won't know his parents. He hasn't got any family.'

Braden sat up a bit straighter and paid more attention. 'What do you mean? He hasn't got any parents? Who does he live with? You talked about his dad when we had breakfast.'

'No, I didn't. You were half asleep, Dad. I said his *carer*. And Mum heard what I said because I saw the look she gave you. Anyway, this is different. I was just helping Lucas when I thought he was hungry, but I'm real friends with Beau already.'

'So what's the carer story?' Braden asked.

'Well, they've just moved to town, and he said he lives with this bloke who wants to be his dad. He said he doesn't want him to be his dad, and he called him a dumb arse. That's where I heard that word.'

Braden was trying to think of a suitable reply when Rory rushed on. 'Okay, so when can Beau come out?'

Nigel leaned forward. 'I don't like him. He smells.'

'Well, he's not your friend, so what you

think doesn't matter, dum—I mean, you can go and watch TV while we're playing football,' Rory said. 'And maybe his clothes don't get washed, so it's not his fault.'

'If my clothes smelled and we didn't have Mum, I'd wash my own,' Nigel chipped in. 'I know how to use the washing machine.'

'You would not, you—'

'Dad, he was going to call me a name again,' Nigel yelled.

The sound of another muffled thump came from the back seat. 'Dad, Rory just punched Nigel,' Petie said.

'Okay, calm down. Thanks, Petie. Rory, I've told you about punching.'

The last six months had seen a change in the family dynamic. Petie was as sweet as ever, but Braden was sure that one day he'd grow out of that too and enter that horrible time between ten and twelve, which Rory and Nigel had just respectively reached.

Almost ten-year-old Nigel had been the difficult child since the boys' mother and Braden's first wife, Julia, had been killed in an accident before Braden had met and married Callie.

It was almost as though a switch had been thrown the day Rory turned eleven. He must be developing hormones or something because he'd been an absolute pain in the butt over the last few weeks, constantly niggling at Nigel. To Nigel's credit, he hadn't flared up as much as he would have done a year or two ago.

'Okay, the first thing is that you pair stop fighting in the back, or no one will be coming to play football. This behaviour, name-calling and punching, is not how we work in our family, and I'm certainly not letting anyone come to play at the station while you two carry on like that. You pair need to show a lot more respect to each other. Got it?'

A couple of mutters came from the back seat.

'I said do you get it?' Braden's voice was louder.

'Yes, Dad.' Two meek voices answered him.

'Good. Second, if you can show me you can behave, Beau can come out one day. But I'm not promising anything, okay? And I'll need to talk to your mum about it. She's been tired lately.'

Pete's sweet little voice came from the backseat. 'That's because you've got twins, and Mum's having another baby. Will we have enough bedrooms when you finish having babies, Dad? Or will we build a bigger house?'

Braden's lips twitched. 'I think we're finished having babies now. When the new one's born, I mean.'

'You might be. You never know what might happen. Penny Wilson told me—'

Braden tensed, but Rory had obviously elbowed Petie. 'Shut up, Pete. We don't wanna hear about all that romance-type stuff. Penny talks about making babies all the time.'

Braden rolled his eyes; his boys were growing up too fast.

The last ten kilometres of the drive into Augathella seemed to take forever. The arguments continued—albeit quietly. Occasional muffled thumps came from the back, and when he finally pulled up outside the school and got out of the ute, he leaned down and kissed Petie on the cheek. 'Off you go, mate.'

Petie ran off happily.

'Right, you pair. I want to talk to you. That behaviour in the car on the way in was unacceptable. I hope you don't behave like that when Mum drives you to school.'

'No, Dad, it was just that—'

'Enough, Rory. I don't want any excuses. I want you to know that from now on, I won't put up with any of that behaviour. I'm going to talk to Mum, and if I find out that you do that when she's driving you to school, there'll be big trouble. And I mean big trouble. Okay?'

Rory and Nigel wouldn't meet his eye, and they lowered their heads, kicking at the dirt.

'Okay?' Braden said.

Nigel looked up and held his eye. 'Dad, I respect that.'

'Rory?'

'Yes, Dad, but it wasn't me.'

Braden refrained from roaring. Instead, he bent down and squeezed both their shoulders. Rory and Nigel maintained they were too big to be kissed by their parents outside the school. 'Have a good day, okay? And be good!'

'Yes, Dad,' Rory said politely. 'We will. Won't we, Nige? And Dad? Don't forget to ask Mum about Beau coming out. You could send her a text maybe,' Rory suggested hopefully.

'We'll see what happens.' Braden gave them a wave, climbed into the ute, and switched his mind to work mode as he headed to the rural store to meet Jon Ingram.

CHAPTER 3
Alice

'Wow, you've got the Audrey Hepburn look going today, Alice. Looking pretty swish.'

Alice smiled at Bec, the team leader at Choice for Youth in Charleville, as she put her handbag on the kitchen counter. Bec was making her first coffee of the day.

'I've got a meeting this morning, remember?' Alice patted her hair. She'd pulled it back into a chignon to match her professional suit.

'Oh, that's right. I really appreciate it. I'm tied up with this other initiative. I can't tell you about it yet, but hopefully, I might hear today. And that's the first time I've seen you with your hair up. You look very sophisticated.'

Alice laughed. 'As long as I look the part. Doesn't feel like me. The last time I turned up at one of the meetings in my youth worker clothes, jeans, and a T-shirt, one principal looked at me as if I had crawled out from under a rock.'

'I appreciate you taking my place today. The local commanders of the three police regions and five high school principals from the school region will be there, as well as the three local schools. With your matching blue shoes and the pearls, the chignon is perfect.'

'Like I said, as long as I look the part. I can take notes for you. I won't have to say much, will I?'

'No, just a presence is fine. You look lovely today, and thanks for going to the meeting for me. Let me know how it goes. I wish I had my news to tell them before then, but I the phone call hasn't come through yet.'

Alice was intrigued. Bec had been very quiet this week, and every time her phone rang, she picked it up immediately.

The meeting went well, and she got back to the office just in time for her lunch break. The last few days had been showery and cold, but the sky had cleared to a brilliant blue when Alice set out for work this morning. Now, it was warm enough to take her cardigan off as she and her co-worker, Tilly Tingle, headed to their favourite coffee shop on the main street of Charleville for lunch. The morning had been busy; the phones had rung non-stop, and the leader of their team at Choice for Youth, Bec, had been closeted in her office most of the time. The three other youth workers, including Tilly's fiance, Jeremy, had headed out to visit a cattle station that had agreed to be part of a program for local youth. Alice and Tilly decided to spend their break at the table outside the coffee shop.

'Thank you.' Alice smiled at the waitress as she brought their baguettes to the table.

'Coffees won't be long. Do you want me to leave the takeaway one until you've finished your lunch?' the young girl asked.

'Yes, please.' Tilly nodded and then looked at Alice. 'I wonder if Bec's off the phone yet?'

Bec had been bursting with excitement all morning. Alice had been going to pump her to see what was happening over lunch, but the call Bec had been waiting for came through as they were about to leave. She waved them off and mimed bringing her a coffee back.

'What's going on, I wonder?' Tilly asked as she reached for her chicken and avocado baguette.

'I don't know,' Alice replied. 'She's been on the phone constantly for a couple of days. Something's happening. At least we know we don't have to worry about our jobs, with Chloe and her group funding the youth centre.'

'That's true. I'm sure Bec'll tell us when she's good and ready.' Tilly lifted her hand and pushed her hair back as the slight breeze caught it. The mid-morning sun glinted on her engagement ring.

'Jeremy certainly didn't waste much time putting a ring on your finger,' Alice said with a smile.

Tilly looked down at the diamond and sapphire ring gracing her finger and smiled back at Alice. 'He reckoned he'd waited long enough. We came down to the jeweller here straight after the Easter camp. Jeremy said he wasn't going to risk any more misunderstandings.'

'You've certainly hit the jackpot there, Tilly,' Alice said. 'He's a top guy.'

'That he is, and yes, we did waste a lot of years, but that's all water under the bridge now. We've sorted everything out. And you know one of the best parts? We're both back living where we want to be.'

'I won't say you're lucky because you went through a tough time until you finally got together, but I am envious.' Alice reached for her coffee cup.

'Envious?' Tilly frowned.

'Oh, don't get me wrong. I'm not in love with Jeremy or anything like that. I'm really happy for you guys. I wish I could find someone like him—a guy with a profession who likes the same things I do. Developing a relationship, falling in love, setting up a home together, and having a family are all I've ever wanted. But I think it's too big an ask. Life's passing me by.'

'What makes you say that?' Tilly put her hand gently on Alice's wrist, and Alice looked away as the beautiful ring sparkled. She wasn't going to take away from Tilly's happiness.

'I saw the happy marriage my mum and dad had. God bless their souls. They're both gone now. They married late in life, and I lost them when I was in my early twenties. I wanted to get married and have kids before I got too old.'

Tilly stared at her. 'How old are you now, Alice? I thought you were that age now.'

'You're my new best friend, Tilly,' Alice chuckled. 'I'll be thirty-three next birthday.'

Tilly's eyes widened. 'Well, that surprises me. Have you always lived here?' she said. 'I don't remember you from high school. You wouldn't have been that far ahead of us.'

'Yes, I grew up out past Allenvale. Dad had a cattle property there. I left high school in Augathella when I was about fifteen. Mum and Dad sent me off to boarding school. Dad wasn't well, and they were thinking about selling the farm. I was an only child and had no interest in the land.'

'Ah, I would still have been at the primary school then. Did you like it? Boarding school, I mean.'

'No, I hated every minute of it,' Alice said. 'I went to a girls' school in Toowoomba. I was a handful back in those days. I did everything I could to get expelled. Sometimes, I think how I was at school helps me understand the kids we deal with. They think they know all the tricks, but I'm usually one step ahead.'

'And you came back to Augathella after high school?'

'I did. I lived in a flat and worked at the IGA here for a couple of years after I lost Mum and Dad. There wasn't much left when the mortgage was paid out on the farm. When I'd saved enough, I went to university and got my social work degree. I did some of it externally and worked to support myself in Brisbane, and then I finished it off at Griffith University.'

'We must have lived in Brisbane at the same time.'

'Maybe. It's a big city, but I did leave for a few years to travel overseas. I've been back in Charleville for about four years now. One day, I'd like to buy a place in Augathella. I love interior design, and I'd spend a lot of time in the garden. Maybe I could buy and renovate houses if I ever get sick of this work.'

'That would be a shame. You love your job, and you are so good at it. I've learned a lot watching you work. Especially at camp.'

Alice chuckled. 'And here was I thinking you were focused on Jeremy that weekend.'

Tilly's cheeks flushed. 'I had time to watch you and Bec work, too. Have you ever had a partner?' Tilly asked. 'I hope you don't mind me asking.'

'I had a close friend at uni who ticked all the boxes, but he wasn't interested in developing a relationship. And I guess there wasn't a spark, so he was right. Then, when I was travelling, I met this Spanish guy in Europe, and we stayed together for a while, but Rafe didn't want to settle down. I told myself we'd stay together; I thought we were pretty serious, but he never wanted to discuss a future together. All he wanted was to do adventurous things: skiing, snowboarding, climbing mountains, etc. I used to sit around and wait for him on the tours, and then he decided he wanted to go and live in Iceland for a while; he was intrigued by volcanoes. That was when I woke up to myself. I knew I didn't love Rafe enough because if I had, I would have gone with him wherever he wanted to go. It was the thought of a relationship I wanted rather than the man himself.'

'It's good that you didn't make the wrong choice,' Tilly said. 'Sounds like we need to do some matchmaking here.'

Alice chuckled. 'No, don't you start. The problem is, there's no one suitable around here. If I want to find someone, I might have to sign up to one of those online sites or move to a city and start going to pubs and nightclubs. Maybe I've waited too long for Mr Right to appear.'

'No, you don't have to do that. I'm a great believer in fate. Someone is waiting for you. One day.'

'One day?' Alice chuckled. 'As long as I don't have to wait twenty years. I'd love a

28

family.'

'It'll happen. Be positive. I thought I'd spend my life alone, but look at me now.'

'You always knew Jeremy was the one?'

'Yes, I did. The few relationships I had in Brisbane just didn't measure up to what we'd had, and Jeremy says the same thing. That's why he put a ring on my finger within a couple of weeks of reconnecting.'

'And a lovely ring it is,' Alice said, pushing away her plate. 'Anyway, as much as I'd love to chat in the sun, I promised the girls at Augathella I'd get some craft samples from the discount store for the ball planning meeting this afternoon.'

'Crumbs, I forgot about that. I hope Nana wasn't too pushy when she talked you into joining the committee.'

'No, I love being involved. Although the time is going quickly, and we have a lot to do.'

'Yes, spring will be here before we know it; the wattle's coming out already. But it's a great initiative. Being on the committee and moving into the aged care facility seems to have given Nana a new lease on life.'

'She was very persuasive when she heard I

like making things.'

'And when Bec told her you also make all your clothes, she was determined to get you on the committee.'

'Are you right to take Bec's coffee back, Tilly?' Alice asked as she stood and picked up her cup and saucer to take back to the counter.

'Yeah, not a problem.'

'I've still got half an hour left on my lunch break, so I'll go back and have a good look at the craft stuff I was looking at when I raced through the other day when I went down to get supplies to top up the lolly jar in the office.'

'Okay, I'll see you back there. Don't worry about taking those cups in.' Tilly reached over and took them. 'I'll take them in while I get Bec's coffee. See you in a while. Bye.'

CHAPTER 4

When Alice left Tilly at the coffee shop, she headed to the huge discount store to look in the craft section for some decals that might be useful for making masks. Gladys had told Tilly that the main task for tonight's meeting was to ensure she passed that on to Alice.

Tilly's busybody grandmother seemed to have taken over the agenda—and the committee—even though she wasn't president or secretary. Callie Cartwright and Sophie Mason had taken on those roles, and now that Jenny Riley's husband was better, Jenny had returned and resumed the treasurer's position.

The discount store was at the other end of the street, and Alice strolled along slowly, enjoying the sun's warmth on her shoulders. It had been a cold winter, and Alice was looking forward to spring, but she knew they still had a lot of planning to do. Tonight's meeting was necessary; it had been a few weeks since they'd last met. Everyone was busy with work and families, and the months had flown by. Working at Choice for Youth with Bec had kept Alice busy, and the time seemed to pass more quickly every week. However, the workload had lessened since Jeremy and Tilly joined the team.

Alice pulled a face; she had more time to herself again. Well, at least she had work to keep her occupied, and the upside of living alone was that she'd have plenty of time to make the masks for anyone who wanted her to. Not only was it time to make some decisions about the ball, but it was also time to make some decisions about her future. Would she stay here, or would she move on in the hope of meeting the right man?

Alice took a deep breath. She walked past the revamped butcher shop, the spicy smell of Smokin' Joe's marinade drifting out into the street. On her way back, she'd call in there for a steak and store the meat in the fridge at the youth centre, ready for her dinner tonight. Some of the marinades in the shop were addictive, especially on these cold winter nights.

Another dinner alone, she thought. Sitting with Tilly and looking at her ring and her happy expression had made Alice realise how lonely she was.

She had a great job and worked with good people, but going home to her empty flat every afternoon, having dinner alone, watching television, or reading a book didn't satisfy her. It's not what she'd imagined for her life. She thought by her early thirties, she'd be happily married with a couple of kids, running them to daycare or school, but here she was, still alone.

With a sigh, Alice walked into the discount store. She needed to give her future some serious thought. She wasn't going to meet anyone here in Charleville. Most of her clientele were already married or in relationships, and everyone else she worked with was still in their teens.

I've got a great job, I'm doing a great job, and I've got to accept that makes me happy enough and stop hoping for the impossible.

The discount store was in one of the biggest buildings in town, and you could find anything there.

'Hi, Cherie,' she said to the young girl at the counter.

'Hi, Alice, how are you?'

Cherie had been one of her successes at the youth centre. She'd run away from home and had struggled with motivation and making ends meet. She wandered into the youth centre one afternoon, and Alice had taken her under her wing. Alice had found her somewhere to live and this job. She'd been working now at the discount store for about three months, and Alice could see the happiness in the young girl's face.

'I'm good. How about you, Cherie?'

'Really good. I've been going to the farm, and I've sorted things out with Mum and Dad. I took on board what you said about families being there for each other.'

'That's great news.' She smiled at the young girl and headed down the back of the store to the craft section.

Browsing along the shelves made her smile. They had decided to have an early Australiana theme for the masquerade ball, and that could mean anything from native animals to the dress of the nineteenth century. Alice stood and looked at the cardboard cutouts of various mammals—a platypus, a kangaroo, and an echidna—and wondered how they could be shaped into masks. There were a couple of very creative, crafty girls in the group. Sophie had surprised her. She'd known Sophie for a long time but hadn't realised what skills she had.

Moving to the end of the aisle, she picked up one of the red plastic baskets and wandered along, picking out a selection of the cardboard faces. There was a brightly coloured parrot cutout on the top shelf, and she stood on her toes, reaching for it.

'Oomph.' A teenage boy trod on her right foot, and Alice yelped as her basket tipped and the contents spread on the ground.

He looked up from his phone. 'Oh, sorry, I didn't mean to do that,' he said, but instead of helping Alice collect the cardboard and cutouts that had fallen on the floor, he took off towards the lolly section at the back of the store.

She shrugged and bent down to fill the basket. Seeing him head that way reminded her she needed to stock up on the lolly jar at the youth centre.

Again.

That was one of her jobs at the centre. In this cold weather, the small wrapped chocolate bars were quickly disappearing, and she suspected that Bec, Jeremy, and a couple of the other youth workers were more responsible for them going down than any of the kids coming after school.

She hitched the basket over her arm and turned into the aisle. There was a wide selection of chocolates and lollies. A movement to her left caught her eye, and she glanced to the side just in time to see the teenage boy who'd trodden on her foot slip a Mars bar into the front of his hoodie. Alice looked away, wondering what to do. Maybe he was putting it there until he got to the counter. She shouldn't make assumptions, but he had looked around furtively before he headed along another aisle. He had a school bag on his back, and that raised her suspicions.

She walked towards the checkout and jumped when the young boy pushed past her. She caught a whiff of stale clothes, and when she looked down, she could see mud on his thin legs. Alice knew most of the kids who hung around town and hadn't seen him before. She might strike up a conversation with him at the checkout, but there was no sign of him when she reached it.

Alice shrugged. Maybe he'd gone to get something else.

She queued up behind an elderly lady paying for her purchases—balls of wool and knitting needles—and listened to Cherie engage the woman in conversation. The young girl had grown in confidence. As Alice reached down to pick up her basket and put it on the counter, an elbow pushed her against it, and she almost stumbled again.

'Hey,' Cherie called out. 'Do you have anything to pay for?'

The same young boy shook his head and kept walking. 'Nope, couldn't find what I wanted,' he muttered before disappearing.

'I'll bet he did,' Cherie said. 'I always doubt them when they come in with a hoodie on.'

CHAPTER 5

'You okay? He fair shoved you, Alice.'

'I'm okay, just in a bit of a hurry. I have to get back to the office. I took too long in the craft section.'

The shop assistant smiled at her and quickly put Alice's purchases into a plastic bag she held open.

'Have a good day, Alice.'

Alice took her change and turned to leave. She looked back at Cherie. 'Have you seen that boy around here before?'

Cherie shook her head. 'No, I haven't.'

'Okay, thanks,' Alice said. 'Have a good day.'

She picked up the bag of craft supplies and hurried to the door. As she stepped out onto the footpath, she looked along the street. The boy was sitting on the seat at the bus stop at the corner.

She glanced at her watch; she still had a few minutes before she was due back in the office, and besides, she had a feeling this was going to be a necessary interaction that was part of her role in the town. She put the bag over her arm, checked that her purse was securely over her other shoulder, and casually walked up to the corner.

The hood was half covering his face, but she knew it was him. As she got closer, she could see the Mars Bar wrapper curled down over the chocolate bar as he scoffed it.

Something wasn't right. He was too young to be out by himself, and she knew he'd shoplifted the Mars bar. As she approached the seat, she walked over to the bus timetable in the Perspex cover to the right of the seat and pretended to look at the bus times.

With a nod, she walked across and sat at the other end of the seat next to him. He barely glanced at her.

'What bus are you waiting for?' Alice asked, keeping her voice even. She looked down into her bag of goodies, so he didn't feel like she was looking at him. 'Have you noticed if the bus to Augathella has come yet?'

He shook his head, but he did turn to her, and she could see his mouth was full as he chewed. When he'd finished eating, he shoved the chocolate wrapper in his pocket and shook his head again.

'I'm supposed to catch the bus home, but I haven't got enough money,' he said.

'Where is home?' she asked.

'Augathella.'

'It's about five dollars, I think. How much have you got?'

He shrugged.

'Not at school today?' she asked. This time, he turned his head and stared at her. Chocolate smeared his lips.

'I had to go to the dentist,' he said.

'Too many Mars Bars?' she asked with a smile.

'No, just a check-up.'

'How did you get down here?'

'I caught the bus.'

'And how come you haven't got enough money to get home?'

His face reddened, and he shook his head for the third time. 'I lost it,' he said.

She stood and walked over to the bus sign again. 'So the Augathella bus leaves at three-thirty. What are you going to do until then?'

'I can't wait that long,' he said. 'I have to get back before the end of school; I'm getting picked up.'

'The bus doesn't leave until after the school bus picks up the kids at the Catholic high school and takes them back to Augathella.'

'That's not on the board,' he said.

'No, it's the school bus,' she said.

His eyes narrowed. 'Are you a teacher?'

'No, I'm not a teacher, but I know the bus schedule. I work with kids. What about your parents? Did they let you get the bus down by yourself?'

He nodded slyly.

'How old are you, mate?'

'Nearly thirteen,' he said.

'Fair enough. So you'll have to hang around town for a while.'

'I guess I do.'

'You want to come back to my work with me?'

His eyes stayed narrowed suspiciously. 'Why would I want to come back to your work?'

'Because I work at the youth centre, and we've got a kitchen and a room with computers.'

His eyes lit up. 'There was a youthie at home.'

'Where was home?'

'Kununnurra.'

'In the Northern Territory?'

'Yeah. Could I wait there until the bus comes?'

'It's a drop-in centre for kids before and after school. And also for those who don't go to school sometimes.'

'I told you I had a dentist appointment.'

'Well, you're quite welcome to come back to the centre with me until your bus arrives.'

'I'm going to be in deep shit.'

'Why?' Alice asked.

'I'm supposed to be back there to get picked up after school. How long does the bus take to go back? It took a long time to get down here.'

'It takes the same time as it did to get here. You'll get back to town about quarter past four.'

'Jesus,' he said.

Alice's eyebrows rose. 'Your parents didn't know what the bus times were? Are they at work?'

'I haven't got any parents,' he said. 'My mum's gone, and *he* took me away and brought me here.'

Alice's chest warmed with sympathy. She'd known he had a story behind him, and she would keep her eye on this kid before he slipped through her fingers. She would follow up on this once she made sure he was safe. 'Are you hungry? How about you come back with me now, maybe have some lunch. And then I could ring your dad if you tell me where he works, and we can get you a lift home to Augathella in time to get picked up.'

'He's not my dad,' he said.

'You have a carer then?' she asked.

'I just live with a guy.'

'A guy. Who's he?'

'Just a bloke.'

Warning bells rang inside her head. 'So maybe I can call him and get permission to drive you back to town.'

'He wouldn't care,' he said. 'You can do what you want, but it'd be good to get back in time so I don't get into trouble.'

'What sort of trouble?'

'Probably cop a hiding,' he said. 'I do all the time if I don't do the right thing.'

Alice stood and put the bag over her arm. 'Come on, I'll take you back, and we'll get you sorted,' she said.

CHAPTER 6

Callie's day at school sped by. Between teaching her class, organising a room for the visitor coming for a sports talk this afternoon, and getting ready for the meeting at Jenna's, she was exhausted.

She combed her hair with her fingers mid-afternoon as Kim Colthorpe came into the staffroom.

'You look tired, Cal. Are you okay?'

'It's just pregnancy tiredness,' she said. 'Plus, I had a cold last week, and that took a bit out of me, and the twins haven't been sleeping well. They're both teething. However, thanks to my gorgeous husband, I got to sleep through the night because he got up and looked after them at three o'clock this morning.'

'Do you think you came back to work too soon?' Kim asked.

'No, it's just normal. The first three or four months of pregnancy is tiring. It was like this for me with the twins, although I was doubly tired then, carrying the two of them.'

'Do you know what you're having this

time?' Kim asked.

Callie gave her a look. 'We sort of do, but we're not saying anything.'

'Fair enough,' Kim said.

'What about you?'

Kim chuckled. 'We're the same. As long as the bub's healthy, I'm happy.'

'It will be like a crèche in town once we all have the babies. As well as us, Fallon, Sophie, and Amelia are having babies, plus we've got the littlies from Laura, Chloe, and Emily.' Callie grinned. 'Must be something in the air out here.'

'It's certainly making the town grow, isn't it?' Kim said, tucking in the chairs at the desks in the front row of the classroom.

'It's the best thing that ever happened to Augathella. Chloe and her group moving here have added to it, too,' Callie said.

Kimberley looked at Callie as she spoke. 'One of the best things for the community and the school was you walking down that road, leaving your suitcases in the ditch, and being rescued by Braden.'

Callie laughed and shook her head. 'Don't remind me. That feels like a different world to me. It wasn't that long ago, though.'

'It wasn't.'

'Packing up and leaving Brisbane and moving out here was the best thing I ever did. It's a wonderful life.'

'Sure is. Now, what's happening with the meeting at Jenna's this afternoon? What time are we supposed to be there?'

Callie looked at her watch. 'Sophie called me before and said Jenna is closing the tea room to the public early this afternoon. So if we could all be there by four, we should be finished by five or five-thirty at the latest, and we won't get home too late.'

'That was good of her. She knows that some of us have got a fair drive home. It'll still be dark by the time we get away anyway,' Kim said.

'Yes, we'll have to watch out for roos on the road,' Callie agreed.

'What about the boys? Are you taking them home today?'

'No, I just texted Braden to remind him about the meeting, and he's coming back through town because he's been out at Jon Ingram's place all day. They've been mustering, so he's going to swing by and pick them up. I might even head off early if that's okay with you. I'm finished

46

with class now.'

'Yeah, that's fine.'

'I've got to pick up some things at IGA and whack them in the car fridge, and then I might head out to Jenna's and rest before we start the meeting. I imagine it will be interesting if Gladys Tingle's there.'

'I think it will be. And she'll be there for sure.'

'She means well, but she's hard to get along with, isn't she? Something must've made her like that.'

'She does. We have to humour her and keep her onside. Make her feel valued. I'll head off now and see you there, Kim. Can you keep an eye out and make sure that Braden gets the boys?'

'Not a problem at all.'

'And before I forget, what do you know about the new boy in Tom Cooper's class? Beau? According to Rory, he arrived last week when I was off sick.'

'I haven't met him yet. I was on a professional day when he was enrolled. He wasn't at school today. I was going to call his Dad and ask him to come in so we can find out

47

where he's up to with his schooling. He started last Thursday. He's come from interstate, and he's almost thirteen. I'm not sure why he didn't go to the high school. There's no mum on the scene, apparently.'

'Rory asked about having him out to play football at home and said he's a really good footballer.'

'Well, kids pick up quickly who's good at what before we even get to know them, don't they?'

'Okay, I'll talk to Braden about it, and we'll have him out.'

Callie picked up her class folder, grabbed her bag, and headed to the Land Cruiser. The twins would be staying at Ruth's while she was at the meeting. Ruth was their wonderful babysitter, who seemed to be babysitting half the babies in town. Callie shook her head. She didn't know how Ruth managed it, but everything was always calm and clean in her house, and the twins were always happy when she picked them up. Even the three boys loved going there; there was always homemade cake and lemonade.

Callie headed to the IGA to pick up some milk to take home, plus four loaves of bread for the freezer. Dinner was sorted, and she added a pack of garlic bread to the basket because she certainly wouldn't feel like cooking vegetables when she got home. Garlic bread and lamb shanks would do them for the night. Or frozen peas; at least the boys would get their greens that way.

She drove out to the highway and turned into the parking area for Jenna's Vintage Tearooms, the most popular eatery in town. A car towing a caravan was driving out, and there was plenty of room left to park.

Callie sat in the car momentarily and took a deep breath, closing her eyes and grounding herself. It had been such a busy day. The baby had moved for the first time today. She hadn't texted Braden yet, but it was one of those moments when you finally realised that you've got another human being in there making little butterfly flutters. Strangely, her eyes filled with tears. Five years ago, if someone had told her she'd be living out on a cattle station, stepmother to three boys, mother of twins, and another baby on the way, she would have told them they were crazy.

Her friend, Jen, from Brisbane, often told her

on the phone that she was a mad woman. 'You had a wonderful life here—sports car, great money, beautiful home on the river. And where are you now? You're out in the red dirt.'

'But, Jen, I'm so happy.'

'I know you are, love, and it's great to see. I was teasing.'

Callie asked her when they were coming out to visit, and Jen had been quiet for a moment. 'Jen? Everything okay there?'

'Yeah, sort of. Phillip is so busy at work, the kids are growing up, and I spend a fair bit of time at home by myself now.'

'Well, if the kids are old enough to look after themselves, why don't you jump on a plane and come out for a visit?'

'Really?'

'Yeah, if the kids stay home, you don't have to worry about waiting until the school holidays. Phillip can look after them for a week or so, couldn't he?'

'You know what, Callie, you're a lifesaver. I think it's just what I need. Are you sure about the invitation? You're not too busy with work and the kids?'

'Not at all, and you still haven't seen the

twins. I'd love you to come out and visit. I know, you could come out for the Masquerade Ball.'

'Okay, you got a deal. I'll do some sussing out with Phillip and the kids, and I'll give you a call in the next week or so. You can tell me all about it then.'

'Sounds good.'

Callie blinked as the sound of a car door closing beside her brought her out of her thoughts. She had almost gone to sleep sitting there.

Sophie was parked beside her. She climbed out and came around to Callie's door.

'You okay there, Callie? I thought you were asleep when I pulled up.'

'I'm just having a two-minute break. It's been a big day.' Callie reached for her bag across the passenger seat, put the car keys in her pocket, and climbed out of the car. She hugged Sophie. 'I haven't seen you for a week or more.'

'I know, it's hard to believe. We've been busy, too, even though I'm not working. Between Kent and Ruby Rose, I never seem to have a spare minute in the day. The highlight of my day is being here without a baby and being able to sit in grown-up company and have a cup of coffee.'

'It will be good company,' Callie said. They looked at each other and chuckled.

'Despite poor Gladys Tingle,' Sophie said as she put her arm through Callie's.

They walked up the stairs to the tea room. Jenna was already sitting at the table with a cup of coffee, talking to Ellie, her offsider.

'The last customer has just left, and I was putting my feet up for a minute,' she said.

'You're entitled to do that,' Sophie said. 'Not like us ladies of leisure,' she chuckled.

'Speak for yourself, Sophie. I go to work,' Callie said with a grin.

'I know you do. I was joking.'

'Hi, Ellie, how are you?' Callie asked.

'I'm good, Mrs Cartwright,' Ellie said.

Callie rolled her eyes. 'It's not Mrs Cartwright, it's Callie.'

'What would you like to drink?' Ellie asked.

'Just the usual, thanks,' Sophie said.

'Me too,' Callie said. 'A skinny cappuccino would be lovely. I want to avoid sugar, though, as I'm trying not to put on too much weight.'

She leaned back and smiled as footsteps pounded on the stairs. 'Here's Gladys and

Beryl.'

CHAPTER 7

The whop-whop thumping of the helicopter landing filled the air and stirred the cattle as they moved around the paddock. Red dust swirled, and Braden ducked his head and pulled his hat down over his face. Jon and Billy Burke did the same.

The new stockman was a quiet bloke, and Braden had tried a couple of times to engage him in a conversation, but he hadn't been very forthcoming. After six hours on horseback and three tea breaks in his company, the only thing he knew about him was that he was from the Northern Territory.

At one point, he spoke to Jon on the side when Billy went off to water his horse and asked about him.

'Good bloke, good references. I knew him briefly when I was up there a few years ago, and I never had a problem with him. He's a bit quieter now than he used to be. I don't know what's happening in his life, but he's one of the good ones, mate. He's also an excellent cattleman, and he has a degree in agriculture, so he's right up there with the latest chemicals and fertilisers. He's taught me a bit already.'

'Okay, that's all I need to know.'

'He's got a kid too. He wants to be done here by three so he can pick him up from school.'

Braden looked up at the sun. 'What do you reckon? We'll be done? I'm hoping to pick the boys up, too.'

'That's not a problem. Once Fallon gets up there, we'll only have that last mob to do. We'll have them all in by two.'

'That's good. I'll go at the same time. Callie's got a meeting at Jenna's. This blasted ball seems to be taking over everything.'

'Sophie's there too. I'm picking Ryan up from Ruth's. Are you going to the ball?' Jon asked with his face screwed up.

'Mate, if you think you're going to get out of going to the Augathella Masquerade Ball, which is going to be the event of the century, you've got another think coming.'

'Someone will have to stay home and mind the kids,' Jon said with a grin.

'Ha ha, didn't you hear that one? Ruth Mason and Beryl are running a crèche. All we have to do is bring a cot, pram, or whatever, and they'll look after all the kids at the venue.'

'Well, I suppose the music will be loud enough that we won't hear all the screaming,' Jon said with a grin. 'I'll offer to help them. I'd rather look after crying babies than dance any day.'

'You got Buckleys, mate.'

Braden looked up as the new stockman led his horse across from the creek.

'Have you heard about this big ball, mate? Will you still be around here in spring?'

'I haven't heard of it, but I should still be around. I'll be here for a while, I hope.'

'Jon told me you've got a young bloke in primary school.'

'Yep.'

'My wife's a teacher there.'

Billy didn't reply, just nodded. Braden caught Jon's eye, and Jon shrugged.

'Okay, guys, back in the saddle. Fallon just came down to refuel, and she's right to go now.'

'She does a good job,' Billy Burke offered.

'She's the best,' Braden said. 'Did you know Fallon up in the Territory?'

'Yeah, I heard about her several times but never met her. She had a good reputation up there, too.'

It didn't take long before the cattle were secured in the home paddock, ready to be collected by the trucks tomorrow. Fallon came over, and Jon introduced her to Billy. She stood on tiptoes and kissed Braden's cheek. 'Hey, Braden, I haven't seen you for ages.'

'I know, we've all been busy.'

'Okay, I'll head back to Charleville and see you at dinnertime. If I get back to town in time, I'll swing by the ball meeting.'

Jon and Braden both rolled their eyes.

'What's wrong with you pair? It's for a good cause.'

'Is it still for the hospital? I heard there was some discussion about that.'

'No, just Gladys Tingle putting her two cents' worth in,' Fallon said. 'It'll get sorted. I'll swing by there if I have time, but if not, I'll come straight home. I took some steak out for dinner, Jon. If you do the veggies, that would be great.'

Braden knew that Billy was watching Fallon and Jon's conversation, but Billy's expression was difficult to read.

'Okay, guys, I'll see you later.' It wasn't long before the helicopter rose above them; the dust settled, and Fallon's helicopter disappeared into the distance.

'Right, guys, we might head into town now. Do you need a lift, Billy? Where are you living?'

Jon looked at Braden. 'Billy's living in the old house down the back of my place.'

'I'll ride back to the house and jump in my car. Thanks for the offer, though, Braden.'

It was the most that Billy had said for the whole day.

'Not a problem, mate. See you around.'

CHAPTER 8

When Alice got Beau settled in the small games room at the back of the youth centre, she went to their office and spoke quietly with Bec.

'I think he's got some issues. I'm not sure about where he's living. I can't get anything out of him, but he's very thin. Plus, he's not very clean, and he claims he needs to get back to Augathella because he's getting picked up by someone.'

'Someone?' Bec's forehead wrinkled in a frown. 'Sounds like intervention is needed, perhaps.'

'Yes, what do you want me to do?' Alice said.

Bec tapped a pencil on the table for a moment. 'You're going up there this afternoon, aren't you?'

'Yes, a little bit later. Tilly and I are going to a ball meeting. Aren't you?'

'I was going to try to get there, but I'm not sure if I'll be able to get away in time. You can't get anything out of him, and we can't get permission, but if he says that's where he lives, we'll get him there, and you can wait to connect with his parents and see if an intervention is needed.'

'Okay, I can do that. I might leave early once he's had something to eat. He's settled down at the computer now. Is that okay with you?'

'Yes, go as soon as you and Tilly are ready. You don't know how long it's going to take to get him sorted.' Bec's face lit up. 'And on a different subject, Alice, I've got some great news.'

'We wondered what was going on. Tell me.'

'Well, you know how Chloe and her group have funded most of our stuff?'

Alice nodded. 'Yes.'

'Well, I applied for an expansion grant, and I was able to say how well it's going here and what an impact we're having on the kids. And provide evidence. It's been approved.'

'Oh wow, what does it mean for us?'

'It means we can open up a centre in Augathella.'

'Oh my goodness, that's fantastic news.'

'More staff and a service for the kids up there. We just have to find a location, and we can get started.'

'Well done, congratulations. That's great.'

'I'm excited,' Bec said.

Alice went into the kitchen and made herself a quick cup of coffee. She pushed the good news to the back of her mind, although she would ask Bec if she could work at the centre up there. She was well placed financially now and had been looking at houses for sale around Augathella.

At the moment, her concern was for young Beau, and she needed to focus while finding out what was going on there. At least she'd have Tilly in the car with her, and there'd be no issues with child protection if anyone queried Beau's being in a car with her.

She made her coffee and wandered through the room, which contained a couple of old lounge chairs and two computers.

'How are you going, mate? Would you like something to eat?'

He turned and looked at her. 'Thank you, but the other lady gave me a sandwich and a drink.'

'That's good. That's Tilly.'

'Yeah, that was her name.'

'I've got some good news for you, mate. We'll be able to give you a lift up to Augathella. We have to go to a meeting up there, so what do you think about that?'

His eyes lit up. 'Oh, that's really good. I won't get into trouble now. Can you drop me at the primary school?'

'Why the primary school?'

'Because that's where I'm getting picked up.'

'Do you go to the primary school or the high school up there?'

'I go to the primary school,' he replied.

Alice was sussing him out. She knew the names of all the staff from a few meetings.

'Who's your teacher?'

'Coops. He said I could call him that, but his name is Mr Cooper.'

'So you're in year six?'

'Do you know the school and the teachers there?' He leaned back from the computer and looked at her.

'I do. I went to school there. I thought you looked older. I thought you were maybe in high school. How old are you?'

He lowered his eyes. 'Almost thirteen. I should be in high school, but we moved a bit.'

'We?

'Yeah, us.'

Alice had enough experience with kids when to know not to push it. 'Okay, fair enough. So do you need to have a drink or go to the toilet before we go?'

'No, I'm ready. What sort of car you got?'

'Government car. Just a sedan, nothing flash.'

'That'll do, as long as I get there on time and I won't get in trouble.'

Alice went into the office looking for Tilly. 'Are you okay with going up now? Bec said it was fine.'

'Yes, I'm right to go. What's the story there?' Tilly asked.

'I don't know, but we're going to do our best to find out. We need to suss out his home situation, I think.'

On the drive up, Beau sat in the car looking out the back window the whole trip and didn't say anything after the first few questions. Alice and Tilly looked at each other and gave up. He wasn't forthcoming, and they were no more informed than they had been when they left. They turned off the highway, and finally, a voice came from the backseat.

'Do you remember where the primary school

63

is?' he said.

'I do,' Alice nodded. 'I'm not that old.'

'Good, just drop me there.'

'Before we do, mate, we need a few more details. What's your last name?'

'Beau Burke.'

'And you're twelve years old, and you've been at school since last week, and you've moved a bit.'

'That's right.'

'Okay, sounds good. Who's picking you up at the school?'

'Why do you need to know?'

'Well, we can't just leave you there in case there's no one there to get you.'

'I told you I was getting picked up. Don't you believe me? Do you think I'm a liar?'

'No, mate. Your safety is our main concern. We work at the centre, and it's our job to look after youth.'

'Okay, Billy is picking me up, and he'll be at the school.'

'What sort of car has he got?'

'A white ute.'

Alice and Tilly looked at each other again. There were probably twenty white utes parked outside the primary school as property owners came to pick up their kids. Taking the bus home took longer, and many of the parents also took the opportunity to do business in town.

They turned onto the main street, then left into Bendee Street, and pulled up next to the school oval. The back was open before the ignition was off, and Beau was off like a shot.

'God, that was quick. I still don't trust him,' Alice said as she quickly opened her door. 'Okay, let's follow him and see where he goes.'

But by the time they were out of the car, there was no sign of Beau; he had disappeared.

CHAPTER 9

Billy Burke sighed as he swung around the corner and parked opposite the sports field. The street outside the school was jam-packed with cars and buses. He'd told Beau this morning he'd pick him up where they lined up for the bus.

The school bell rang as Billy climbed down from the ute, tucked his phone and keys in his back pocket, and headed along the street towards the school's front gate.

Beau had had one of his quiet mornings as they'd eaten breakfast together, and Billy had kept his phone handy all day, waiting for the school to call about a meltdown. To his surprise, the boy had lasted all day at school. At Kununurra, the phone call had been a daily event, and in the end, it was easier to keep Beau home from school and take him out to the cattle stations where Billy was working. That's when the social worker became involved and told him that action would be taken.

Moving to Augathella gave them a chance for a new start. Picking up the job with Jon Ingram and the bonus of a house at the back of the property to live in had been a godsend.

All they had to do now was get Beau settled in. They'd arrived too late in the season for him to play in the local junior rugby league team; there were only a couple of games left before the end of the season finals. Beau was already talking about joining next year. His love of NRL football bordered on obsessive, but at least it gave them something to talk about. Apart from that, there was little conversation. If Billy asked Beau, "Did you brush your teeth?" he was rewarded with a dismissive glance. At least watching football on television gave them something to do together in the evenings and on weekends and occasionally—very occasionally—resulted in a conversation of more than two sentences.

Billy found caring for the young boy hard, but he'd had no hesitation when Mary called him home. A pang of regret lodged in his chest. If he'd stayed in Mt Isa, he might have established a relationship with Beau before his sister left them.

Billy hadn't seen him since he was a baby, and now he was his only family. Being the sole carer of an almost teenager had him on a steep learning curve, but Billy was determined he would make a success of it.

Beau had always lived in Mount Isa, and with everything else, the move to Kununurra had messed with his head. Setting up home here in southwest Queensland in another unfamiliar place had been the final straw, and Billy had tried to talk to Beau about seeing someone and getting help to deal with his feelings. That was if you could call sitting in front of the television with no response talking.

He'd had nothing to do with kids, so he had no idea what to do. The social worker in Kununurra has been intrusive, and it was one of the reasons Billy had thought about moving south. When he'd heard that Jon Ingram was looking for a stockman on his new station out of Augathella, the decision was made. One phone call, and they were on their way.

Billy knew Beau was a good kid—he always had been; Mary had kept him in the loop. It was just a matter of finding the right place, the right friends, and getting him back on track.

As Billy rounded the corner near their arranged pick-up place, he paused as a stream of kids in school uniforms came pouring through the front gate. Three female teachers stood near the buses, and each looked at him as he walked past.

'That's not bad to see,' he thought. They were keeping an eye on anyone they didn't recognise.

He approached the woman who appeared to be in charge. Her badge said Mrs Colthorpe, Deputy Principal.

'Good afternoon, Mrs Colthorpe. My name is Billy Burke. I'm here to collect Beau.'

He never tagged himself as a carer, stepdad, or uncle because Beau seemed to prefer that. He refused to call Billy anything—not uncle, not Billy. They were still getting used to each other. Billy knew he'd gone a bit soft on the kid, but hell, he'd been through a lot for a twelve-year-old.

'Hello, Mr Burke. It's good to meet you. He's not catching the bus home today?' the deputy principal asked. 'He hasn't come out yet. Ah, here's his class now.' She gestured to a group of students around Beau's age.

'Yes, he was a little bit upset when he left this morning, and I've been half-expecting a phone call from you all day, but he obviously settled in okay.'

They waited until the group lined up, and Mrs Colthorpe frowned. 'He's not with his class.' She turned and spoke to the woman on the other side of the gate. 'Penny, have you seen Beau Burke?'

'He's not here today,' the woman replied. 'When I checked the roll at drama this afternoon, he was marked absent.'

Mrs Colthorpe took his arm and pulled Billy to the side, away from the chatter of the children lined up.

'Are you sure he got the bus this morning, Mr Burke?'

'He didn't get the bus today. I had to come to town, so I dropped him off and watched him go in the front gate. He must have misunderstood where I said I'd pick him up. I'll call him. Hopefully, he's got his phone on.'

Billy pulled out his phone and thought carefully about what to say when Beau answered. He didn't want to sound angry because then he would take off. He'd done it before in Kununurra, and the first time he went missing for two days, the authorities got involved, and that useless social worker had taken him on her caseload. The last thing he wanted was for Beau to go into care. Mary had been very explicit: Beau was to stay with Billy until he reached eighteen. Luckily, she'd been to see a solicitor, and it was all in black and white.

He waited for the phone to pick up, but it went to voicemail. 'I'm here to pick you up, mate. Where are you?'

He waited for his phone to ring or ping with a reply, but it stayed silent.

'What does she mean he was marked absent?' he asked. 'Absent from drama class? He'd hate that.'

'No, it means he wasn't in class when the roll was marked this morning. Maybe he's on the premises, but it appears he didn't stay with his class for the day. When I was on playground duty at lunchtime, I didn't notice him on the football field either. And that's where he's spent most of lunch and recess for the week or so he's been here.'

'He loves his football,' Billy said, reaching in his pocket for cigarettes before he realised it was inappropriate to light up here, and besides, he didn't have any. He'd given them up a fortnight ago, after one night when Beau accused

71

him of being addicted. He'd managed not to smoke for two weeks now, but the stress of wondering where Beau was had had him reaching for one without thinking.

'Do you have any idea where he might've gone? Does he have any other friends in town?' Mrs Colthorpe asked, concern etching her features.

'We don't know anyone yet. His only friends are at school, if he's made any, that is. Shit. I watched Billy go into school this morning, so his well-being is then the school's responsibility.'

'Yes, it is,' she said. 'Wait a moment, please, Mr Burke.' She hurried across to one of the other teachers.

As he waited, he sent Billy a text.

I'm at the bus lines, mate. Where are you?

As Mrs Colthorpe came back over, Billy glanced down at his phone.

'It looks like he's out of range,' he said. There was a red symbol beside his message saying not delivered. His concern ramped up a notch. Beau's phone was always fully charged, and he always had it on.

'Come into the office with me, please, Mr Burke.'

They walked through the front door and along a corridor. The deputy principal stopped and tapped on a door marked Principal. She opened the door and took a step so she was just inside the door.

'Sorry to interrupt, David, but we've got a bit of an issue here. One of our new students is apparently wagging today, and we don't know where he is. I have his father with me.'

'Come in, please,' a male voice responded.

'Mr Burke, this is David Foy, our relieving principal,' the woman said.

A short man with a ruddy complexion stood, came around the desk, and held out his hand to shake Billy's.

The look of disdain on his face when he shook Billy's dusty hand filled Billy with instant dislike.

'It's good to meet you, Mr Burke. I was away last week when your son enrolled. I'm relieving here at the moment, and I like to meet our parents. Now tell me what's happened.' He gestured to a table with four chairs around it.

Billy ran his hands through his hair before he pulled out a chair and sat down. 'He's had a head start. If he's decided to take off again, he could be halfway to Brisbane by now. I'd like to know why the school didn't let me know he wasn't here.'

'Don't worry, we'll sort this out. Kim, who's Beau's teacher?' the red-faced man turned to the deputy as he wiped his dusty hand on an ironed handkerchief.

'Mr Cooper,' she replied.

'I'll ring the staffroom and see if he's still here.'

He walked to his desk and picked up the phone. 'Coops, could you come to my office, please? Don't worry. It's not serious.'

He put the phone down and came back to the table. 'He's on his way.'

'Nothing serious?' Billy held back his temper as best he could. 'It's damn serious, mate.'

'I didn't want my teacher to think he was in trouble.' His stare was cold.

'I don't give a flying fig what he thinks. My boy is missing. And we're wasting time sitting around here.' Billy stood up so quickly his chair fell over.

Mrs Colthorpe stood and put her hand on his arm after he'd picked up the fallen chair. 'Calm down, Mr Burke. He won't be far away. We'll look for him as soon as we talk to Mr Cooper. I'll ask him to get a group of teachers together as soon as we establish what he knows. There are a few things we can do.'

'Like what?' Billy asked.

'Just give us a moment,' she said. 'Can I get you a cup of tea or some water?'

'No.' Billy turned to head for the door, but it opened before he reached it. Another teacher walked in.

'Mr Cooper, we need to know as much as we can about Beau Burke's routine,' Mrs Colthorpe said. 'It looks like he's wagged school, and we're unsure where he is this afternoon. This is his father.'

Billy didn't correct her.

'I'm sorry, Mr Burke,' the male teacher said with a frown. 'He told me yesterday he wouldn't be here today because he was going to the dentist, so I marked him as sick.'

Billy frowned. 'No, he wasn't going to the dentist.'

'Who has Beau palled up with, Coops?' Mrs Colthorpe had taken control, and the bloody principal sat there, flicking through papers on the table. Billy held back his anger, but it was hard. If they didn't get moving, he'd go looking himself. The problem was he had no idea where to look.

Mr Cooper was still frowning. The more he heard, the more Billy wondered if this school had been the right choice. 'He's very friendly with Rory. They're together every day before and after school, at recess and lunch.'

'Hopefully, Rory's still out there. He was on the oval waiting to be picked up. We can ask him what he knows,' Kimberley gestured for Billy to follow her.

'Right. I'll come with you.' Billy followed her down the corridor.

CHAPTER 10

Braden parked behind the school on Nelson Street, on the other side of the sports oval, and cut through the vacant block to the oval. There was never any parking out the front, and the boys enjoyed kicking the football around while they waited for him.

He spotted the boys near the shed at the side of the oval. They were kicking a football around with a boy he assumed was Rory's new best mate.

He whistled and waved to let them know he was there. Rory raced over ahead of Nigel and Petie, and the unfamiliar boy followed them across to where Braden waited.

'Hey guys, ready to go home?' He looked at the newcomer. 'You're new to the school, I hear, mate?'

'Yes, sir,' the boy said.

'Dad, I talked to Mum before, and she said that Beau could come home with us this afternoon. He'll get picked up later.'

Braden raised his eyebrows. 'She didn't message me about it.'

'She said *I* could tell you, Dad.'

'Okay, I'll send her a text now.'

'No, there's no need. She said Beau could come today, didn't she, Nigel?'

Nigel looked at Rory, his eyes narrow. 'Yeah, if you say so. I wasn't listening.'

'Is that okay with your parents, Beau?' Braden asked.

'Yeah, I can go to your place and get picked up later.'

'Okay. I'll still text Mum and see what she's arranged.'

'Don't you trust me, Dad?' Rory held his gaze steadily.

'I do. You have never given me any reason not to. I'll send her a quick text to see the pickup arrangement.'

Braden took out his phone and texted Callie. He waited for her to reply, but there was no answer. With a shrug, he said, 'Okay, Beau, come along. We'll sort out how you're getting collected later.'

As long as he didn't have to drive back into town to bring him back. Braden had a few jobs to do when they got home. As they drove home, he was unsettled. It wasn't like Callie not to let him know, and he wondered whether he'd done the right thing, but he knew she'd had a busy day. Rory had been very persuasive, and as he'd said, his son had never given him any reason not to trust him.

Half an hour later, they turned into the drive and approached the house.

'Wow, not a bad place.'

Braden glanced in the rear-vision mirror. Beau's eyes were wide.

'We've got a great area at the back too, great for playing footy,' Rory said. 'Dad's mowed it and put goalposts in too. Wait until you see it.'

'How about some afternoon tea before you play footy?' Braden said when the ute was in the shed. 'There was some cake left after I packed your lunches this morning.'

'That would be good,' Beau said. 'Thank you, Mr Cartwright.'

The boy's manners were fine, even though he looked a bit scruffy. He seemed like a nice enough kid.

'Rory and Nigel, show Beau the bathroom. You can all have a clean-up, and I'll get some afternoon tea and milkshakes.'

The three boys threw their bags in the

breezeway and shot up the hall, Beau behind them; he must have left his bag in the ute. Rory still had his football under his arm. Braden whistled as he went into the kitchen.

CHAPTER 11

Screams of laughter and the barking of three dogs drifted across the house as the boys played football. Petie was out there, too, but Braden knew he'd be more interested in playing with his dog, Apricot, than football.

He was about to head out to the shed when the landline rang in the study.

'Hi, love, it's me,' Callie said. 'I'm about to leave town. Is there anything we need?'

'Not that I can think of,' Braden said.

'I've picked up some garlic bread for tea and thought we could have frozen peas with the lamb stew. I put some potato and carrots in it. Can you check the slow cooker for me? I'll be about half an hour.'

'I will. How come you're calling the landline?'

'I tried your mobile, but it rang out.'

'That's strange.' Braden walked back to the kitchen and picked it up off the countertop. 'Ah, I must have switched it to silent accidentally. Looks like I've had a few missed calls.' He frowned. 'A couple from the school. I'd better call them and see what's up. Did you see my text, Cal?'

'No, sorry, I haven't looked at my messages. What's up?'

'Rory said it was okay for this new mate of his to come out this afternoon. He said he squared it with you.'

There was silence on the other end of the phone. Callie's voice was firm when she finally replied.

'Then I'll have to have a talk with Rory when I get home. We didn't have any conversation about it.'

'He lied to me.' Braden's jaw tensed.

'If he told you that he'd spoken to me and I gave him permission to have a friend over this afternoon, I guess that's what you call it. I didn't see him through the day, and I certainly haven't spoken to him.'

'Little bugger,' Braden said.

'So what's happened?' Callie asked. 'Is he there?'

'Yes. Beau came out of school with them. Rory said his carer was going to come and pick him up afterwards. Wait until I get my hands on that little—'

Callie cut him off. 'There will be a consequence for the lie, but if this boy has no friends, I guess Rory was trying to do the right thing. Leave it until I get home, Bray. What's he like?'

'He's got manners. He said his pleases and thank yous and called me sir a couple of times, which made me feel old. They're out playing footy now. I've been keeping an eye on them through the kitchen window, and everything *seems* fine.'

But Callie said, 'I can hear the "but" in your tone.'

'He's pretty scruffy and very thin. Between you and me, he looks a bit neglected.'

'Have you given him something to eat?'

'Yes, he had two pieces of cake, and I made them chocolate milkshakes. And some fruit.'

'Did he say anything about his parents?'

Braden shook his head. 'No. I'll call the school. Maybe that's what they called about.'

'Okay, it sounds like Rory's a good kid. I'm coming straight home.'

'Yep, but I hate that he lied to me about talking to you.'

'Leave it till I get there, and we'll sort it out.

It's getting dark now, so I hope he told someone he was coming to our place. Otherwise, they'll be worried when he doesn't go home.'

***

Billy was more than worried; he was trying to hold his worry in, and the more he did, the more anger took over. By the time they'd gone out to the front of the school, there was no sign of this Rory or his father. And now, half an hour later, Beau still hadn't turned up. The school hadn't been able to get in touch with the boy's father either.

'I think it's time to call the police,' Kim said. She'd insisted he call her that, and she looked as concerned as he was, which made Billy worry more.

He ran his hands through his hair again. 'Give me a minute to think about it. I'm trying to think where else he could've gone.'

His words were interrupted by the ringing of the phone on the principal's desk.

'Yes, thank you,' David Foy said. 'Please put him through.' He listened carefully and nodded sagely. 'That's excellent news. Thank you very much. Yes, Mr Burke is here now looking for him. I'll put him on in a moment after

I tell him.' He put the phone down on the desk and looked at Billy. 'Beau is out at a property half an hour out of town. He apparently went out there after school to play football.'

Billy kept his face expressionless as relief flooded through him. At least Beau was safe, although he would be in trouble when he got his hands on him.

He calmed down before he took the phone from the principal; that wasn't the way to handle a situation like this. One thing that the social worker had told him was to stay calm and try to talk things out rationally with Beau.

'Braden Cartwright would like to talk to you and organise for Beau to be collected,' the principal said.

Billy sat up straight. 'Braden Cartwright?'

'Yes, that's Rory's father.'

'I worked with Braden at the Ingram's property today.' His heart rate slowed as relief built. 'He's obviously in good hands.'

'I can't comment,' the red-faced principal said. 'I don't know them.'

'He's one of the best,' Kim said. Billy caught the disgusted look she shot the principal's way.

'You couldn't ask for a better place for him

to be,' Mr Cooper said. 'The Cartwright boys are top kids, and Callie, their stepmother, is actually a teacher here at school.'

'I'll put you onto Mr Cartwright now, and you can work something out.' He looked at the other two teachers. 'We'll give Mr Burke some privacy.'

Billy took the phone as the three teachers walked out of the room. 'Billy Burke here. Braden?'

'Yeah, mate, it's me. I didn't think I'd be talking to you again so soon. Apparently, there's been a bit of a mix-up, and we've got your young bloke out here. I suspect the boys cooked it up themselves.'

'So I believe.'

'Do you know your way out here? Do you know where we are?'

'No, I don't,' Billy said.

Braden gave him directions on the way to head out of town. 'After you turn at the intersection, turn right there, and then you'll see the *Kilcoy Station* sign, mate. It's getting late. We've got plenty for dinner. Stay for dinner and meet Callie and the rest of the family.'

'Thanks. We'll talk about it when I get there.

I'll see you in a little while.'

CHAPTER 12

As Alice locked the car, she spotted the school bag on the back seat.

'He's gone without his bag,' she said.

'Tilly, you go that way across the football field, and that'll put you up in Nelson Street. I'll go from here along the front of the school, and we'll meet up at the corner. He has to be here somewhere. I want to make sure he's okay. Did you think he looked neglected?'

Tilly nodded. 'Yes, and his clothes smelled dirty. There's something not right there. I wonder if he's really getting picked up. We know his name and what he looks like. If we don't find anyone, I'll go and see the school principal and see if they know anything. Actually, Kim's out front now on bus duty, so I'll have a chat with her if we don't find him.'

'I might have a chat if we do find him,' Alice said.

'I'm off.' Tilly scooted across the football field as Alice made her way towards the school. There were all manner of vehicles parked along the road, and she recognised lots of faces as she glanced into them. Trying not to get into conversation, she waved and kept walking. Kids she used to go to primary school with now had their kids in kindergarten, and she ignored the pain that hit her chest. She was here to look for someone else's child, and it wasn't the time to regret not having kids yet.

She walked to the corner carrying the bag, but there was no sign of Beau. Tilly was walking towards her and raised her hands as if to say she hadn't seen him either. Alice stood there for a moment, amazed at how quickly the school crowd had cleared. The last bus had left, and the teachers went back inside. Now, there were only a couple of cars parked around the corner.

'How about we walk down to Main Street and see if he's gone there? The library's open, and he could have gone to IGA or the football field,' Alice said.

'Or he could have been picked up,' Tilly said.

'Yes, but they would probably have hung around looking for his bag.

They each took a side of Main Street, and half an hour flew by as they looked in the shops and the library, and Alice checked out the park.

Tilly looked at her watch. 'I'm going to have to go, Alice. 'I promised Nana I'd go with her and Beryl to the meeting.'

'That's fine. I'll call into the school office and drop his bag in. I'll see you at Jenna's.'

As Alice headed for the front gate of the school, a voice came from behind. 'Hey, who are you?'

She turned around to see a tall guy in dusty work pants standing with his hands on his hips. A battered Akubra hung from one hand. She frowned and walked over to him.

'Excuse me, were you calling me?'

'Well, no one else is around, is there? Do I know you?' he said. 'What I want to know is, what are you doing with that bag?'

She looked down at Beau's bag still in her hands and frowned. 'Why? What's it to you?'

'Because that's Beau's bag. It's got his initials on it. See, B.B. And you're holding it,' he said.

'Beau?'

'Yes, Beau. What are you doing with his bag?'

'He left it in my car. I'm looking for him to make sure he gets his bag back and that he's okay.'

'And why wouldn't he be okay?' he asked. 'Exactly who are you, and why did you have Beau in your car?' His eyes narrowed suspiciously.

He took an instant dislike to her. Her hair was perfect, her makeup flawless, and her navy blue suit wasn't creased. She looked just like one of the social workers from Kununurra, the ones who'd caused all the trouble for them.

Her eyes widened, and she drew in an audible breath. 'My name is Alice Templeton, and I work at Choice for Youth in Charleville.'

He'd been spot on. 'What's Choice for Youth?'

She stared at him, and Billy felt as though he was being assessed—and found wanting—as her gaze slowly raked him from head to toe. His eyes stayed on her, and he kept his expression bland.

What was that woman's name from Kununurra? This one even looked like her, not in looks but in the way she checked him out. She was younger and better looking, but still, she got his hackles up.

'I bumped into him, literally, in a discount store in Charleville around lunchtime.'

'Charleville?' Billy groaned out. 'What the hell was he doing in Charleville?'

'You tell me,' Alice said. 'Beau was not forthcoming when I questioned him.'

'Not forthcoming, hey? Who gave you permission to question him?' Billy said.

'I saw a boy who was quite distressed, obviously hungry, and he told me he didn't have enough money for the bus to get home after his dental visit.'

'Dental visit? He wasn't going to the dentist.'

'Are you sure?' she said calmly.

'Unless he made the appointment himself and jumped on the bus this morning, but he wouldn't have had any money to pay for it. He hasn't even got a Medicare card yet.'

'And why would that be?' Alice asked. 'Is he your son?'

'I don't think that's any of your business,' he said. 'Now give me his bag, please.'

'Not until I know who I'm talking to and if you actually have a right to take his bag.' Her chin shot up, and her eyes challenged him.

CHAPTER 13

With a smile that had no friendliness, the guy held out a hand stained with grease. 'Billy Burke. Who are you?'

'Alice Templeton.' Alice winced as his dirty hand held hers; his grip was so firm it hurt. If it weren't for his dour expression and the aggression coming off him in waves, he would've been a very good-looking man. Her face had heated when he'd caught her checking him out. Snug-fitting, dusty denim moulded muscular thighs, and a tight navy blue T-shirt showed well-developed arms and broad shoulders.

Alice cleared her throat. 'Okay, let's start at the beginning. I work down in Charleville. At lunchtime today, I happened to be in a store and came across Billy. A few minutes later, when I went outside, he was sitting at the bus stop, and he was a bit upset because he didn't have enough money to get home.'

She didn't mention the shoplifting.

'How the hell did he get to Charleville? He was supposed to be at school. I dropped him off this morning.'

For the first time, his expression softened. 'I'm sorry if I appear curt, but I've just spent the last hour looking for him.'

'You and me both. He shot out of my car when I parked. I wanted to make sure he was telling the truth and was really getting picked up.'

'He was, but he wasn't here. I know he wasn't at school today, and I know where he is now, so everything is okay. He's safe. Did you offer to bring him here?'

'It's fine.' Alice nodded. 'It was discussed with my boss, and I had permission. There was another youth worker in the car with me. It was either that or leave a kid sitting in a town with no money, no food, and looking quite vulnerable.'

'So you decided to be a good Samaritan and take him wherever he wanted to go.'

'Yes. He was distressed because he had told me he'd been to the dentist, had gotten the bus down, and had spent all his money. He didn't have enough money to get home, so I drove him back. However, as soon as I pulled up, he got out of the car and took off, and he left his bag behind. Where is he now?'

'Well, he's pulled a fast one again. I came

94

here to pick him up, but he decided he was going to go home with one of the kids to play footy apparently.'

'Are you sure he has?'

'Yes, I've spoken to the guy who took him home.'

'May I ask you one thing, Mr Burke? Are you his father?'

'Is that any of your business?' he said.

'It is, actually. I'm a youth worker down in Charleville, and I have some concerns about Beau's care.'

His jaw tightened, and he glared. 'Well, Miss Templeton, that's none of your business. I can assure you that Beau is fine. He's well cared for, he gets fed, he's got a bed to sleep in at night, and he's going to school. And that's about the best anyone can do at the moment in these difficult circumstances. So how about you butt out?'

'No, I'm not quite sure about this. Do you know that in my position, if I have concerns about the care of a child, it's mandatory that I make a report?'

'A report? Why the hell would you need to make a report? Beau wagged school, he's been

95

caught out, and he's going to face the consequences. He's safely home, thanks to you, and I appreciate that. I'm pleased that you looked out for him—it could've gone very badly if he hadn't met the right person. So thank you, Miss Templeton. However, I can assure you that there is no need for you to worry at all about Beau.'

'I'll be sure of that when I see him,' she said.

'Is it really any of your business?'

'I've already told you, and yes, it is my business. And if necessary, I will make that report. I want to be sure that Beau is alright.'

He sighed visibly and took a deep breath. He reached out and picked up the bag from the ground. 'Okay, you're from Charleville, so you probably don't know the local people, but he's gone to *Kilcoy Station* and is currently in the care of one Braden Cartwright, who I have just spoken to on the phone. I'm going out there to pick him up now. And between you and me, he's going to face some consequences: one, for wagging school; two, for lying about going to the dentist; and three, for putting himself in a position of not being able to get home and relying on the goodwill of someone; and four, for not waiting for me when he was supposed to get

96

picked up and deciding to play at someone's house, which is about thirty-five kilometres away from where we are now.'

'I know exactly where Braden Cartwright lives,' she said, 'and I do know the Cartwrights. They're very good people.'

'So I've been told. Thanks again for looking out for him, but that's the end of the matter.'

'I'm still not satisfied,' Alice said. 'I won't make that report, but I would like to meet with you again and see where you're living.'

His eyes fixed on hers, intense. 'If that's what it takes, we can meet. Do you have a phone number?'

'Yes, I do. Please text me your phone number, and I'll reply. Then I want you to tell me where you live. I'll come out and see where you are, and if I'm reassured, I'll leave you in peace.'

He removed his phone from his back pocket and showed her the number.

'Okay? I'll text you and make sure that's right.'

'For God's sake, is there anyone you trust?' he said.

'Not when the care of children's involved.' She put the number into her phone, texted him and nodded when his phone pinged.

'Good.'

'Happy now, Miss Templeton?'

'Yes, I am. I'll be seeing you soon, Mr Burke.'

CHAPTER 14

Alice was seething. She had met some rude and uncooperative people in her life—it went with the job—but never had treated anyone her with the disdain that Mr Burke had.

She took an instant dislike to him. He was rough and ready, and his manners needed attention.

He put his Akubra on and then tipped the brim. 'I'll wait for your call, Miss Templeton.' He turned on his heel and headed to a white twin cab ute that had seen better days. She stayed there watching until he drove around the corner. At least she knew Beau was okay; he'd been fine with the Cartwrights. But there was a lot more to the story, and she would get to the bottom of it. Why had Beau taken himself off to Charleville?

Alice was thoughtful as she drove to the meeting at Jenna's tearoom. She thought she was early, but when she looked at the clock on the dash, it was already heading towards four-thirty.

She turned off the highway to a full car park. Chatter and laughter met her as she climbed the steps up to the beautiful tea rooms. Every time

Alice came here, she appreciated what a great job Jenna had done. When she'd grown up in Augathella, the old house had been a local eyesore. When Reg had lived there, the weatherboards had been faded and rotting, and the block had been covered with long grass.

Now, it was a pretty cottage. Jenna's Tea Room sign was written in old English script, and the roses that Jenna had planted the first spring she'd been there now tumbled down the railing of the steps and across the fences—the smell of early blooming jasmine carried on the breeze. The whole feel of the tea room made you want to relax, smell the roses, and let calm fill you.

That wasn't a bad idea, Alice thought to herself. For some reason, she'd let that Billy Burke really upset her. She wasn't satisfied that things were okay, but there were processes to follow. Perhaps she was wrong; hopefully, she was.

Conversations filled the room as she walked into the tea room. There were about a dozen women already sitting at the long table along the window that overlooked the rose garden.

'Hi, Alice, come and sit down,' Callie called out. 'We're about to start the meeting.'

Tilly was sitting beside her grandmother on Callie's other side.

Alice smiled at Gladys Tingle and Beryl as she sat opposite them in one of the two vacant chairs.

'I thought I was early, but the time got away,' she said.

Gladys smiled, which was quite out of character. 'Hello, Alice. How did you go with those samples you were going to bring up for the masks?'

'They're in the back of the car,' Alice said, not letting on that she had totally forgotten about them after encountering Billy Burke. 'I'll run down and get them.'

'Leave it until we're ready to talk about the masks later in the meeting.' Callie caught Alice's eye, and Alice knew that Gladys would take over when she brought the craft supplies up.

'Okay, I'll just grab a coffee now,' Alice said. Maybe that would help settle the trembling feeling in her arms and legs.

Ellie took the last of the coffee orders, and when she and Jenna brought the drinks over, Jenna joined the meeting, and Callie tapped her spoon on the side of her teacup.

'Are we ready to start?' Callie sat at the head of the table. 'Ladies, thank you all for coming. Let's get this meeting started. Thank you to those of you who emailed me with items to discuss. I've got a bit of an agenda here. I'll read it to you, and if there's anything that you think we don't need to talk about today, just let me know when I finish, or if there's anything else that we've missed, please let us know. We've only got an hour. I know it's a terrible time in the afternoon, but it suits those of us who work. Plus, thank you to Alice and Tilly for driving up from Charleville.

'Right. The first thing that we really need to talk about—actually, no, instead of going through them one at a time, I'll list the things that I've got, okay? I've got fundraising—that is, who we're fundraising for—the ball theme that we discussed, and we need to talk more about that. We need to talk about who's eligible to come to the ball. Plus, the venue and catering.

'Is there anything else that's pressing that we missed?'

'We need to discuss the ticket price, but that will depend on the fundraising goal,' Amelia Foley said.

'I'll add that to the agenda,' Callie said. 'It's a good point, thanks, Amelia. So, how about we start with fundraising, as that will drive a lot of what we do? Jenny? Your thoughts?'

Jenny Riley had worked as treasurer on quite a few other committees over the years, and she had been appointed treasurer at their first meeting. She'd had to take some time out when her husband was ill, but she was back on board and raring to go now that Tom was well again.

'We had decided that it would be for the hospital to develop the maternity wing, but since then,' Jenny looked across at Laura with a smile, 'Dr Harry tells me that the government has looked at recent data. Because of the increase in births locally, they've agreed to increase funding for the hospital next year.'

'So what you're saying,' Gladys said, 'is that the need for funding for the maternity wing is not so pressing.'

'Yes, that's correct, Gladys.' Jenny looked around the table. 'What does everyone think?' A robust discussion took place, and especially as there were so many pregnant women in the group, some good points were raised, but the general consensus was that more funding for the maternity wing was not really needed at this point.

'Maybe we could just have a ball and not have it for fundraising,' Beryl suggested tentatively.

Gladys turned sideways and gave her an icy look. 'The point of the ball is to raise funds for the community. Isn't that right, Callie?'

'As chair, I'm open to all suggestions. It's then up to us all to vote as a committee. It's not my decision,' Callie said. 'What does everyone think? Has anyone got any other suggestions for worthy fundraising? Alice, what do you think? You know a fair bit about the region. How do we compare with Charleville and some of the other local towns with funding for various initiatives?'

Alice thought for a moment. 'Well, there are sporting clubs, schools and the hospital. Our aged care facilities can always do with more funding. I don't know if anyone else has got any other thoughts.'

Chloe put her hand up, and Callie nodded. 'Chloe?'

'Well, I can tell you that at the moment, we've got some initiatives in place for the football club and the cricket club.'

'What about the school, Callie? Is there anything that they need to purchase?' Jenny asked. 'Something in the way of resources or equipment rather than staffing.'

'Well, we're pretty lucky. We've just received more funding from the federal government rural school bucket, and we're pretty right with sporting equipment again, thanks to Chloe and her group for their kind donations over the last twelve months. The only thing I can think of is maybe some cultural activities, but that means we need to fly in people like illustrators, authors, and motivational speakers. There is a need for motivational speakers in education, particularly for teachers who are suffering a little bit of stress. I know of a really good speaker who talks about depression and balancing your work-life, and I think something like that would be worthwhile. But I know the speaker I have in mind charges a four thousand dollar fee plus accommodation and travel costs to get him here.'

'It sounds like a good possibility,' Sophie said. 'Our teachers are important to us.'

'Alice, what about the youth centre? I've heard a whisper that there are some changes there,' Rosie asked.

Bec was late to the meeting, and Alice hesitated, unsure whether the expansion was public knowledge or not. To her great relief, footsteps sounded on the stairs, and Bec came through the door.

'Hi, everyone, sorry I'm late.'

'Great timing,' Gladys Tingle said. 'We just asked Alice a question, but she seems reluctant to answer.'

Alice turned away and rolled her eyes. Given her mood this afternoon, it would be easy to snap at Gladys. She was an astute old bird, but she could be painful to deal with if things didn't go her way. Tilly, her granddaughter, seemed to cope with her snarky words, but Alice didn't have the patience these days. Her patience was all expended on the local youth.

And Billy Burke.

Bec sat down, and Ellie got up to get her a coffee. 'Flat white?' she asked quietly.

'Yes, please, the usual,' Bec said. 'What can I help you with, Gladys?'

Gladys gestured for Callie to answer.

'We're looking at the fundraising recipients from the ball,' Callie said. 'The hospital's not in need of funding for the maternity section anymore. We talked about a few possibilities. The school has no need, apart from maybe some mental health funding for staff professional development. Sophie asked about your youth centre, Choice for Youth—'

Gladys interrupted Callie before she could finish. 'But *I* don't think it qualifies as it's in Charleville. This ball and all funds raised are for the *local* community.'

Bec caught Alice's eye as she leaned back, and her grin was wide. Alice knew that she was about to spill the news.

'Well, everyone.' Bec looked along both sides of the table. Alice noticed Gladys lean forward, her eyes gleaming as she prepared to pounce on any words she didn't want to hear. 'I've got some very good news for Augathella this afternoon. I finally received the phone call I was waiting for today and got the final confirmation that we're opening a branch of Choice for Youth up here in Augathella.' She turned to Alice. 'Thanks for not spilling the beans before I arrived, Alice.'

There were some positive nods and murmurs around the table. Gladys' mouth dropped open as she stared at Alice with narrowed eyes.

Alice bit the inside of her cheek so that nothing rude came from her mouth, but she could still think about it.

'That's great news,' Jenny Riley said.

'So, if the centre's starting here, what's being funded?' Beryl asked.

She was certainly getting gamer these days, Alice thought.

'Well, mainly leasing a building and getting some more staff, but we won't have anything to put in it, you know, like computers, lunchroom facilities, meals for kids on the weekend,' Bec said. 'The sooner we can resource it and start activities up here, the more it will benefit our local youth. At the moment, we can bring some of our resources up from Charleville, but that will probably mean opening only a couple of afternoons a week.' She looked at Alice, who nodded. 'But if we knew that more funding was on the way, we could split the resources equally across the two centres until we had funding for the Augathella centre on its own.'

'Well, I think that's a great idea.' Callie smiled widely. 'Thanks so much for letting us know the details, Bec. Now that we know the youth centre is opening, I think we should provide some funding for all the things you might need to make it a top-notch place. What do you think, everyone?' Callie asked.

Gladys Tingle shook her head. 'I don't think so. We need to be looking at the aged care facility. We need stuff there. There are not enough books to read in the library. The food isn't very good, and none of us have televisions in our rooms. We have to go out to the lounge to watch television.'

Everyone was quiet as they considered that.

'Okay, well, we've got two possibilities to consider,' Callie said. 'Let's not decide tonight. We don't have to do it until we start printing tickets and publicising the ball. We don't really need to say what it's for yet, so let's give it a couple of weeks until our next meeting. That gives everyone a chance to think about what they prefer.'

Sophie caught Callie's eye across the table with a small smile, and Alice thought to herself that Callie had handled that very well. She could teach Alice how to be diplomatic. The image of that damn stockman came back to her—again— and she closed her eyes.

Why wouldn't Billy Burke stay out of her

head?

The rest of the meeting was spent discussing the other items on the agenda, and just after five, Callie stood. 'Okay, everybody, that's been a great meeting. Thank you, Alice, for bringing those craft items. It's given us some fabulous ideas. Thank you, Sophie, for offering to sew some costumes. So, if everyone puts some thought into what we discussed today, when shall we have our next meeting?'

'A fortnight,' Jenny Riley suggested.

'Does that suit you, Jenna, if we have it at the same time? Four o'clock back here?'

Jenna nodded. 'All good.'

Callie raised her hand to quiet the chatter that had started. 'One last thing. I forgot to thank Jenna for providing the coffee for everyone and not charging us. You didn't have to do that, Jenna.'

'That's my contribution,' she said. 'Plus, if we have raffle prizes on the day, I'll be happy to donate some lunches and afternoon teas for that, too.'

'We didn't even talk about raffle prizes,' Sophie said.

'Next meeting. I'll send out an agenda in

about a week. If you think of anything, email or call me.' Callie said. 'Okay, everyone, thank you so much for coming and for all the ideas. We've made great progress today. This way, we'll all be home before dark.'

Alice stood and waited for Tilly to say goodbye to her grandmother before they drove back together. Being in the company of the other women and thinking about things broader than her job had calmed her a little, but a niggle of anger still tugged at her as she thought about Billy Burke. Her first job tomorrow would be to make an appointment with him.

CHAPTER 15

It was almost five o'clock by the time Billy turned at the *Kilcoy Station* sign. He looked around with appreciation; the cattle were fat and in top condition, and the paddocks were lush and green. The drive down to the house was about a kilometre long. As he approached the red brick building, he could see the boys playing football in a paddock that looked like it had been marked out as a football field.

As angry as he was with Beau, he was pleased that he had actually connected with some kids. Good kids, by the sound of things. When they'd stayed at Mt Isa for a few months after Mary's funeral, Beau had turned into a loner. Then, the move to Kununurra had made that even worse.

Even if Beau had wagged and lied to get here, seeing him playing football with kids his own age tempered Billy's anger.

A little bit.

Beau was still in big trouble and would suffer consequences for what he'd done. They'd sit down tonight and have a very serious talk.

Billy had decided to let it go this afternoon. This wasn't the place to discuss it, but Beau had to be taught about risk-taking behaviour.

Billy also wanted to find out what happened in Charleville with that woman who had bailed him up this afternoon. He was still angry about the way she'd spoken to him as she vocalised her doubt in his ability to care for Beau.

What did she know about their circumstances, and how dare she form an opinion?

God knows it had been hard enough, but he was doing his best. He was trying to deal with a battle he hadn't had time to fight. The situation was caused by his dropping Beau off at school early so he could meet Jon at the rural store. Maybe if he'd told Jon he had a kid, he could have made different plans. He and Beau had kept to themselves since they'd moved into the old farmhouse about five kilometres from the Ingrams' new house.

But one thing that Billy wouldn't do was rely on other people. They needed to be independent. They had each other, and that was all that mattered. If Beau had gone off the rails for one day and someone thought he looked neglected, dirty, and hungry, well, that was something that he'd be addressing, and he wouldn't hold back in telling Beau what she had said.

The boys heard his ute approaching, and a football bounced on the road in front of it as four boys ran over. At the same time, Braden came out of the big shed to the left of the house. Billy drove over to the shed, parked there, and reached over to shake Braden's hand.

'Braden, was your son at school today, or did he wag school with Beau and go to Charleville?'

'What? Charleville?' Braden said. 'Hang on a moment.' He hurried out of the shed, and the next minute, he roared, 'Rory Cartwright! Get your butt in here right now. By yourself.'

Braden was speaking so loudly Billy could hear every word. 'I don't want you to lie to me. I want the truth, mate. Did you go to school today?'

'Yeah, Dad, you saw me go. You dropped me off there, and you picked me up.'

'But did you *stay* at school all day?'

'Of course I did. Where else would I go? There's nothing else to do in town.'

'Are you telling me the truth, mate?'

'Yes, of course I am.'

'Okay. Do you know if Beau was at school today?'

There was a long silence.

'Okay,' Braden said. 'You guys just keep playing. We'll talk about this later when Mum gets home.'

'Have you talked to her yet?' The boy's voice quavered.

'Yes, I sure have, and there are going to be consequences. That is one thing we don't do in this family—tell lies to get our own way. Outside now, Rory. We'll talk more later.'

Braden came back into the shed, shaking his head. 'It sounds like we've both had a bit of a day with the kids,' he said.

'Yep,' Billy replied.

'Apparently, Rory *was* at school. He tells me he was, and I tend to believe him. I don't know what else has happened. Do you want to talk about it while you're here?'

'No, I'll sort it out with Beau once we get home. I'm sorry if he's been a nuisance, Braden. I didn't expect that to happen.'

'No, not at all. They're having a good time, and I'm sure I did similar things when I was a teenager.'

'And me too. It's the beginning of hard years for both of us, I would say.' Billy ran his hand through his hair. 'Thanks, mate. I owe you. Beau's gone off the rails today, from what I can tell, but he ended up safe, and I'll sort it out with him. The best thing is seeing that he's made some friends and is interacting with others like a normal kid. There hasn't been a lot of that.'

'Mate, I'm guessing you've had some tough times,' Braden said. 'If you ever need to talk, I'm a willing ear. 'There's a beer fridge in this shed and many a problem has been sorted here.'

'I appreciate it, mate. I might take you up on that. Looks like you've got some experience with kids.'

'Speaking of which, here they come, and two of them are looking very sheepish,' Braden said quietly. 'Is Billy okay, or would you prefer Mr Burke?'

'God, no,' said Billy. 'Billy is fine.'

Braden put his hand on the tallest boy's shoulder. 'Billy, This is my older son, Rory. He's the same age as Beau, I believe, and this is Nigel, and this is Petie.' He looked proud when each of the boys shook Billy's hand. 'Good manners, boys, thank you.'

'What time is Mum coming home?' Nigel said. 'I'm hungry.'

'Mum will be about half an hour,' Braden looked at Billy. 'I think I told you Callie's a teacher at the school, but she had a meeting about this fundraising ball this afternoon. She'll be home in a little while, and she'll have our other two kids with her.'

'Two more? You've got five kids all together?' Billy said, running his hands through his hair.

'Yeah, mate. Our youngest are eighteen-month-old twins.'

'And I think I've got my hands full with one.' Billy looked over at Beau, who was looking very nervous. He went over and put his hand on his shoulder. 'Good to see you home safe, mate. We'll have a chat later, fair enough?'

Billy felt Beau's shoulders tense as he continued speaking, but he didn't move away. 'I'm actually Billy's uncle, but he's now my adopted son, and we're learning how to get along together.'

'Our boys can help him. Callie is their stepmother, and we all had lots of learning to do.'

'Mum left her bags in the drain, and they

nearly drowned. Dad saved them, and they fell in love. Callie and Dad, that is, not the bags. We got a new Mum,' Petie said.

Billy got the general gist of the story and smiled.

Braden gestured to the shed. 'It's still light enough for the boys to play a little bit longer. Can I offer you that beer? I've got light beer.'

'I'd appreciate that, mate.'

'And think about what I said. Dinner's on offer, too.'

'Can we stay for dinner?' Beau said. 'Their mum is a really good cook, and it's lamb night.'

'We have to get home, Beau. We've got some talking to do, and I've got an early start again tomorrow.'

'Maybe you could stay the night here,' Petie piped up. 'We've got plenty of spare beds.'

Billy laughed and ruffled his hair. 'Thanks for the offer, mate.'

'Maybe Beau could come out and stay with us one weekend,' Braden offered.

'We'll have a chat about that. Sounds good,' Billy said. He glanced over at Beau, who had a grin from ear to ear. It was the happiest he'd seen him look for at least twelve months.

Maybe he'd go easy on him tonight. If it was okay, they might stay for dinner. It might mellow Beau a little bit more.

CHAPTER 16

Callie took the drive home slowly. It was that awful time of the afternoon when she hated driving—the sun had set, but it wasn't quite dark. The fading light made it hard to see kangaroos on the road, and she also had to dodge corrugations along the way. At least the twins were well-behaved. Ruth had given them early dinner and bathed them. She was an absolute gem.

It was almost six when she turned into the driveway and wondered whose ute was parked outside the shed. The big shed lights were still on as she put the car away in the garage on the side of the house. She rolled her eyes as the washing flapped on the line.

'Thanks, Rory,' she muttered. As she got out of the car, a sharp twinge pulled in her lower left side, and she caught her breath.

'Just the baby stretching my muscles,' she reassured herself. She stood there until the pain eased and was gone as quickly as it had come. The washing could stay out for the night; it would be damp again by now; at least Rory—or someone had hung it out.

She'd hoped that Braden would have heard the car, but there was no sign of him.

'Come on you, pair, bedtime.' Seeing they'd had their dinner, it would only be a matter of a bottle each, and they could go straight to bed. She lifted the small bag of groceries and the two strollers out of the back of the Landcruiser; the twins were too heavy to carry at the same time now. She strapped them in; her bag and school stuff could wait until later.

From the breezeway into the house, she could hear laughter, and couldn't help her smile as the sound of a Nintendo game drifted down the hallway. She hoped they'd done their homework. Although, by the sound of things, that young fellow Beau was still here, and she assumed the car must belong to his father. The talk with Rory could wait until after they'd gone.

When the twins were out of the stroller and sitting happily in the old-fashioned wooden playpen in the corner of the kitchen, she lifted the lid of the slow cooker. A tantalising aroma of lamb and herbs filled the kitchen. The casserole was bubbling along gently. She turned the cooker off and flicked the kettle on, ready to boil water for the peas and pasta. She headed up the hallway and stuck her head into the games room. Petie called out and raced over, throwing his arms around her legs.

'Hi, Mummy. Where's our twinnies? You didn't forget them, did you?'

She ruffled his hair. 'No, sweetie. They're in the kitchen.'

He took off down the hallway, and Callie smiled. Petie would sit for ages, playing peekaboo with the twins around the playpen. The smile disappeared when she walked into the games room; she was disappointed with Rory's behaviour. It was so out of character; she couldn't remember him ever lying before, and that made her wonder about this new friend.

Rory and Nigel were sitting in their beanbags, and an unfamiliar boy was sitting on the floor between them.

'I'm home,' she said loudly over the noise of the game.

'Hey, Mum,' Rory took his eyes off the screen for a second. His eyes met hers and skittered away as she raised her eyebrows.

'Perhaps you'd like to introduce me to your new friend, Rory.'

'Sorry, Mum, this is Beau. You were off school when he arrived last week.'

'That's right. I haven't met Beau yet.'

The young boy pushed himself to his feet and, to his credit, came over to her. 'Hello, Mrs Cartwright. It's very nice to meet you. Thank you for letting me come out to your house this afternoon.'

Nigel jumped up and said, 'Dad's invited Beau and his dad for tea. Is that okay with you, Mum?'

Callie nodded, although the last thing she wanted was visitors. She was exhausted. 'If Dad actually did say that, they are more than welcome to stay.'

Rory looked at her again and then looked away.

'I'll go over and see Dad and meet your dad, Beau. Ten more minutes, boys.'

'He's not my dad,' Beau said.

'Oh, okay, I'll go and see them then,' Callie said, wondering what the story was.

Petie was still playing peekaboo with the twins, and she smiled as laughter and giggles filled the kitchen.

'Can you stay there, please, Petie? I'm just

going out to the shed to see Dad. Dinner's nearly ready.' She wouldn't put the peas on until she knew if the boy and his father were staying.

'Yes, Mummy.' Petie giggled as Munro reached out and grabbed his hair. 'Ouch, that hurt, Munnie.'

'Don't get too close. He's getting very strong.'

Callie headed out to the shed. Braden and an unfamiliar guy were sitting in the little den he had built at the back of the shed near the beer fridge.

'Hi, Callie, I thought I heard you drive in. We were just about to come inside. This is Billy Burke,' Braden said.

Billy, who was a very good-looking man, came over and extended his hand.

'Please excuse the cattle dirt on me, Mrs Cartwright,' he said, his voice deep and low.

'Callie, please. It's fine. I know you've been working with Braden and Jon all day. I'm more than used to it, so don't worry.'

'Callie, I've invited Billy and Beau for dinner. Is that okay with you?'

'Yes, of course it is. I met Beau. Of course, you're more than welcome,' she said to Billy with a wide smile. 'I've boiled the water for the peas, the lamb's ready to go, and I'll get the kids to set the table while I put the twins down.'

'I can do that. Let them keep having a good time. They've been really well-behaved this afternoon,' Braden said.

'Beau is very polite,' Callie said to Billy.

He chuckled. 'When it suits him. It is good to see him having a good time and being polite. I'm sure you've heard about the dramas today at the school. Braden and I have been talking about it. Beau wagged school. I'll be having a good talk with him when we get home.'

'And we'll be talking to Rory later, too,' Braden said.

'Please stay for dinner, Billy. It will be too late once you drive home.'

'Thank you, I appreciate it,' he said. 'I'm sure Billy will be, too, because I'm not much of a cook.'

Callie hesitated. 'So I don't put my foot in it, may I ask about Beau? He said you're not his dad?'

'That's right. I'm his uncle, but I do have legal custody of him. My sister passed away last year.'

'Oh, I'm so sorry to hear that.' Callie leaned over and kissed Braden's cheek. 'I'll go and put the twins down. Can you pop the frozen peas in the water before you set the table, please, love?' She walked to the door. 'It's an easy tea here tonight, Billy.'

CHAPTER 17

'They're good people, aren't they, Billy?'

Billy stared ahead, his hand clutching the steering wheel. He was looking out for roos.

It was good of Braden and the others to suggest they stayed the night, as it had been late by the time they finished dinner and chatting.

'They are.'

It was quiet again for a few minutes as they approached Augathella and then headed west past the airfield.

'We need to have a chat.'

'Yeah, I know.'

Billy forced his hands to relax on the steering wheel. 'I'm not going to write you off, mate, but I want you to listen to me. Your mum put you in my care, and you are my responsibility. If you had any idea of the worry I had today when I thought I hadn't looked after you properly and then I'd lost you, you might understand what I'm trying to do. Now tell me why you went to Charleville?'

'I don't know. I don't like the school.'

'But you've got mates there. You seem to be

getting on really well with Rory and his brothers, and I know you're playing football, too.'

'Yeah, but I can't do the work, and I feel stupid when I can't do it, so I don't want to be in class.'

Billy's heart clenched. 'You missed a lot of school when your Mum was sick. We can sort something out about that, mate. Nobody has to know.' Thinking about Mary made his throat ache. She should be here with them, watching Beau grow up. All was quiet for a while as they left Augathella and then headed west towards Jon and Fallon's place.

Billy broke the silence once he had his emotions under control. 'I don't want to lose you, Beau. Because Mum—'

His voice trembled. 'Because Mum made you promise to look after me.'

'Yeah, that's a big part of it, but also because you're my nephew, and I'm the one who's going to look out for you as you grow up. I want to make sure I do the right thing. I was worried that I hadn't been doing it properly for you.'

'You do alright.'

Billy supported himself with his hands on the steering wheel, and his shoulders sagged in relief. 'We are sort of poking along alright together, aren't we, mate?'

'Yeah, we are. Can we watch the footy tonight?'

'I think we might have missed it, but we can watch the replay on my phone.'

Silence reigned again as they navigated the twenty kilometres of dirt road, past Alan Humphreys' station and down to the Ingram's place. Billy turned his head as Beau said something. 'Sorry, mate, I missed that. What did you say?'

'I said I'm sorry, Billy.'

Emotion clutched at Billy's chest. Maybe Beau doing this had forced a change in their relationship and in both of their attitudes.

'It's okay, mate.'

'Am I going to have any punishment?' Beau asked.

Billy shook his head. 'No, I can see what caused it. I'm just pleased that someone looked after you down there and helped you get home.'

He might be pleased about that, but he certainly wasn't looking forward to meeting with that woman again. He felt like something on the ground under her shoe when she looked at him.

'Alice was nice, Billy.'

That was the first time Beau had used his name since he picked him up.

'Oh, she looked after you well, but she reminded me of that social worker up in Kununnurra.'

'No, she was nicer than her. But I've got one thing to confess.'

Billy tried not to smile. 'What else did you do, mate?'

'I left my bag in her car.'

'I know you did, and she gave it to me.'

'Oh, sweet,' Beau said.

CHAPTER 18

Alice left it until late on Monday afternoon to ring and make the appointment to talk to Beau's carer the following afternoon. She thought a lot about it over the weekend and wondered whether she overreacted. Still, she reminded herself that Beau had left Augathella without permission, travelled on a bus to Charleville, wandered around town, had no money, and had shoplifted a Mars Bar before he realised the error of his ways.

The call was brief and to the point. Billy Burke agreed to meet at the time and venue she suggested—the small meeting room off the bistro in the pub at Augathella. They could have met in Jenna's tearooms or in the room that Chloe had at the side of the department store, but Alice had a feeling that this was going to be a difficult interview, and the room at the pub was more private.

On Tuesday afternoon, before she drove up to Augathella for the meeting, Alice went to the ladies' room at the youth centre. She pulled a face at herself in her bathroom mirror as she carefully outlined her lips with the soft pink lipstick that always made her feel confident. She couldn't understand why her stomach was in knots; for goodness sake, she had done dozens, if not hundreds, of interviews with carers, parents, and families over the past four years since she had been working as a youth worker.

For some reason, Mr Billy Burke, new to town, unsettled her. It wasn't only because he was such a good-looking guy; his confidence and brashness almost intimidated her.

Almost.

Even in his dust-covered stockman clothes and with his Akubra on, it was clear he was a fine-looking man. What had most drawn her attention were his clear, dark blue eyes surrounded by long black lashes. His face was rugged almost to the point of roughness, but that was relieved by the laughter lines fanning out from his eyes. His nose was straight, and his lips were full. If she was honest, even with his ruggedness, he had the sort of looks that you often saw in advertising campaigns.

She shook herself again. His appearance and attitude were no reason to have herself tied in knots.

Her primary concern was supported by the notes she'd made. She identified that Beau had shoplifted. He had told lies about having permission to go out to the Cartwright house, and he hadn't been forthcoming with her when she asked about his situation. Normally, she would've done a notification alone when she had concerns, but she hadn't discussed it with Bec because she knew that Bec would have encouraged her to do it. But there was something about Billy Burke, and the sadness that he carried, had made her decide to give him a chance before she did a notification. Not only would she talk to him, but she would also get his permission to talk to Beau at the school.

Alice had thought long and hard about what to wear that morning before she went to work.

In the end, she chose a pair of black trousers and put on a long-sleeved olive green T-shirt and a set of black chunky beads. Hair up or hair down? She'd compromised and swept her hair back into a high ponytail. There, she looked professional but casual, and by the end of the day working in the youth centre, she would be even more crumpled and relaxed.

Now, she took one last look in the mirror and was happy; her expression was calm and composed. She *felt* professional, and she *looked* professional.

Now, all she had to do was hope that Billy Burke would be as professional within the interview situation as she wanted him to be.

***

'No problem, mate. I'll keep an eye out for him. Hey, I'll ask Fallon to cook some pikelets, and he can come to us. Is that okay?

'Thanks, I'll bring him over before I go. I shouldn't be in town too long. I hope, anyway.'

Billy had mentioned his trip to town this afternoon with Jon when they knocked off from drenching the cattle. He'd given Jon a bit of an explanation about Bea and why the meeting was important.

'I can't afford a whiff of trouble, mate, and that social worker or youth worker or whatever she is looks like trouble.'

'Not Bec Hunter?' Jon said. 'She's great. No need to worry there.'

'No, no, her name's Templeton or something.'

'Yeah, I know Alice. What are you worried

134

about?'

'She looked officious, and she looked like she would follow things to the letter of the law.'

'Well, I guess she does have to follow procedures and policies, but if there's one word that I wouldn't apply to Alice Templeton, it would be officious. She's a young, gentle soul. She gets on well with everyone in town. I've been to a few functions that she's been at. She's working with the girls on this ball, too.'

Billy shrugged. 'We'll see. I'm talking to her in an official capacity. I think most people are different when they socialise.'

Jon took his hat off. 'Going to head to the shed. You got time for a coffee, mate?'

Billy glanced down at his watch. 'Yeah, the school bus won't be in for about ten minutes, if he's on it.'

'Troubles with the boy?'

'He took himself out to the Cartwrights the other afternoon after we'd been mustering. Turned out well. Braden looked after him, and they made me feel very welcome.'

'You couldn't get a better family,' Jon said. 'And the boys will be a good influence on Beau if he's struggling a little bit. You guys have had a tough life by the sound of things. Do you mind if I ask you? Are you his dad?'

'Oh, hell no,' Billy said. 'I've got no kids.' He split a grin for a second. 'Not that I'm aware of anyway.'

Jon chuckled. 'So you're a carer?'

Billy shook his head. 'No. Beau is my sister's son. Mary passed away last year.'

'I'm sorry to hear that, mate. It must be tough. His dad?' he asked. 'Tell me if I'm being too nosy.'

'Mary was a bit of a girl in her time, and she always assured me that she didn't know who Beau's father was.'

'It's not on the birth certificate.'

'No, and now any chance of ever finding out is gone.'

'How does Beau feel about that?'

'Mary talked with him when she was sick, and she said he was fine with it. He showed no interest, but if he ever does, there's really nothing I can do about it. Mary was only seventeen when she had him, and I was living away. I'm a fair bit older than she was. She was living in Cairns at that time, doing bar work, and she said she had no idea who the father was. As much as I hate to

136

think about it, I think that might've been a way she supplemented her income.'

'Was she sick?'

'Yeah, she knew she was dying. She had cervical cancer. She let it go too late, and by the time it was discovered, it had gone too far.'

'Sorry, mate, you've had a rough trot.'

'It has been hard, Jon, but I'm determined to do the right thing by young Beau. Problem is, I can't get him to respond to anything. The only thing he's interested in at all is football. We watch the football at night on that TV in the house, and sometimes he forgets who he's with and cheers and says things to me like, "Oh, did you see that try?" or "What's the ref doing?" I can honestly say that's the only conversation we have through the whole week.'

'And now you're worried about Alice? What worries you there?'

'She told me she could do a notification because she was concerned about Beau's well-being.'

Jon stared at him. 'But, mate, you look after him well.'

'As well as I can. The little bugger won't shower and won't wash his hair, so he always looks scruffy, and he's always been thin, always a gangly almost-teenager. I didn't fill out till I was in my early twenties. So I know he looks like he's not getting cared for well, but he eats like a horse. I found out the full story about him wagging school the other day. He jumped on the bus and went down to Charleville, and that's where Alice caught him. And then that same afternoon, he lied about having permission to go out to the Cartwrights. By the time Braden rang me, they were already out there.'

'Okay. Like I said, don't rush back, and if you need some time out after the meeting, we can keep an eye on Beau until you get back. We haven't got much on, and that new young ringer needs to work by herself a bit more. If there's anyone with her, any chance to be a bit lazy, I don't know if she's going to last.'

This time, Billy chuckled. 'I noticed that. I wasn't going to say anything yet.'

'What about Beau? Has he ever done the Cattle Cadet program?'

Billy shook his head. 'I don't know. I've asked him. He won't tell me what he's done. If football's mentioned, you can get something out of him.'

'Okay, I might have a chat with him one afternoon. I might "accidentally" bump into him out in the paddock or something.'

'I really appreciate that, Jon. Thanks, mate.'

Alice reached the pub with enough time to compose herself before the meeting. She parked the car and walked into the bistro. Sean, the manager, was polishing glasses behind the bar and looked at her with interest. He had already asked her out a couple of times, but Alice had politely declined.

'Hey Alice,' he said. 'How are you going?'

'Good, thank you, Sean. I've booked the room next to the bistro for a meeting.'

'Yeah, Billy is in there already, waiting for you.'

Alice glanced down at her watch. 'Already? He's early.'

'Yeah, he wandered in here about twenty minutes ago.'

'Okay, thank you.'

'What can I get you to drink?'

'Is your coffee machine on?' she asked.

'Sure is.'

'Just a flat white, thanks.' She pulled out her wallet.

'No need to worry about it. Coffee's on the

house this afternoon—a coffee to celebrate you coming up to run the youth centre here. The whole town is talking about it. Alice Templeton, coming home.'

'Really?' Alice wondered if Sean was working up to ask her out again.

'Yeah. You're a local, born and bred. So the story goes.' Sean turned to the coffee machine.

'But you've been here a long time,' Alice said. 'You were working here before I left town, weren't you?'

'I was working out on a property at Adavale back in those days. Look, you go in. I'll bring your coffee in.'

Alice swallowed and straightened her shoulders as she walked to the door on the other side of the bistro. Billy Burke was sitting at a table, drumming his fingers—little finger to thumb, little finger to thumb, making a repetitive drumming sound.

'Good afternoon, Mr Burke,' she said.

He looked up, and his eyes widened as he took in her appearance. 'Good afternoon, Miss Templeton.'

'Please call me Alice,' she said.

'Are you sure?' he said.

'Of course.'

'You look much more like an Alice today,' he said.

'What is that supposed to mean?' She bristled.

'Well, the lady in the suit and the pearls and the bun was definitely Miss Templeton, but I think you're an Alice today.'

Alice forced a smile and pulled out the chair opposite. That was some sort of start, anyway.

'So, thank you for meeting me here.'

'I won't say it's my pleasure because it's not,' he said.

Her eyes widened at his brusque response. She put her bag on the floor, leaned forward, and clasped her hands on the table in front of her. His fingers were still drumming on the table.

'Do you mind not doing that?'

'Doing what?' he said.

'Making that noise with your fingers,' she said. He looked down as if surprised that he was doing it.

'Sorry, nervous habit.'

'You're nervous about meeting me?' she said.

'No, not nervous. I can't see the point.'

Alice sighed. She would stay professional and not be cranky.

'Well, Mr Burke, we need to talk about Beau. I need to be sure that he's being well cared for. The situation last Friday didn't really reinforce that for me. Can you tell me what your relationship is with Beau?'

He looked up from his fingers, which had stopped moving on the table, and his eyes were on her—those blue eyes that she found so compelling on Friday, even when they were full of anger, frustration, and worry. Her mouth dried, and she dropped her gaze. It was ridiculous having that trembling feeling from a client across from her in a professional setting. Maybe it was just nerves.

'Well, Alice,' he said. She looked up and held his gaze again. It was the right way to approach this.

'I'm Billy's uncle. My sister Mary had him when she was seventeen. She never told me who the father was, and there's no name on Billy's birth certificate.'

'So there was no chance of a father taking him?' she asked carefully.

'No. Mary got sick and died about a year

143

ago.'

'I'm sorry to hear that.'

'Yep, it was a hard time. I stayed with her for the last four months, and I saw Beau's grief when he realised that his mother wasn't going to live. Until then, he was always a good kid, but when Mary finally passed away in the hospital, he went inside himself, and he's barely interacted with anyone since then. He's healing, though, steadily. And that's why I'm so pleased to see that he's established a rapport with the football team here and the Cartwright boys.'

'So, is there a formal relationship between you?' she asked.

'Yes,' he said, his voice deep and steady. 'It was all organised before Mary passed away. I've adopted Beau, and it's all legal.'

'And how does he feel about that?'

Billy shrugged. 'Beau's just learning to feel again, I think. It's been less than a year since he lost his mum. We've moved twice in that time, and he's just finding his way. I'll be honest with you, Alice. I've had nothing to do with kids. I knew him when he was a little tacker, and it's a whole new learning experience for me. So what exactly is your problem, apart from him taking off and telling lies, which I'm dealing with?'

'Well, I'll be honest. I was concerned about how thin he was. I was concerned about the state of his clothes and, to put it bluntly, he didn't smell very clean. And that screams neglect to me. Mr… may I call you Billy? If you're calling me Alice?'

'Yes, you may.'

Her heart went out to him as he lowered his head and ran both hands through his sun-tipped hair. He was in need of a shave, but the attractive stubble on his face was quite appealing. She deliberately kept her eyes away from the navy-blue T-shirt that snugly moulded his chest.

Before she could speak, the door opened, and Sean came in with a cup of coffee.

'Here you go, Alice.'

'Thanks, Sean. I appreciate it.'

By the time the barman left the room, Billy had composed himself.

'Okay, let's talk about your concerns about Beau,' he said. 'One, I find it hard to get him to have a shower. I'm lucky if he has one every three days. But short of stripping him down and putting him in the shower myself, which I'm not prepared to do yet unless you say it's absolutely necessary, he's going to look a bit grubby at times. We haven't got a washing machine out at the Ingram's place yet, and I've been hand-washing stuff, but no matter how often I put his clean clothes in his room, he picks up the same dirty clothes every day. And by the time I try to wash them, he's wearing them. And as I said, I'm certainly not going to hold him down and strip him off. Our relationship is too fragile for that. I'm taking it very slow and easy, Alice, as I'm sure you can probably understand.

'As for his size, the little bugger eats like a horse. I'm at IGA every two or three days, stocking up on fruit, meat, and vegetables. And trust me, he eats properly. He burns it up. He never stops. If he's not in bed asleep or sitting at the table eating, he's outside kicking a football or running around. He burns it up. Now, you can either believe me, or you don't. So that's the situation. I'm doing my best.'

Alice nodded and looked away, then reached down and picked up her coffee cup. As she lifted it to her lips, their eyes met again.

***

Sean tried to catch her attention as she left the pub. Billy Burke had lifted his hat, put it on his head, tipped the brim to her, turned on his heel, and left about five minutes ago. It had taken her a good five minutes to calm down; nothing had been achieved in the fifteen-minute meeting.

Billy had explained the things she'd been concerned about with Beau, and she guessed she could understand and probably accept them. He explained the background, and it wasn't her business to check whether he was telling the truth or not. She was the youth worker, and she was concerned. She needed to do a notification, and the powers that be would investigate whether Billy was a suitable carer for his nephew.

At times during the talk, his sincerity had shown through, and she could sense frustration in his words as he explained the difficulties of dealing with a young boy who didn't want to do as he was told. She was still in two minds, but she knew that most of her hesitation about doing a notification was because of Billy Burke himself.

Something about the man attracted her—whether it was his sincerity and willingness to take on a twelve-year-old boy and be a single dad or simply that she found him attractive. It was doing her head in.

She stood and tucked her chair in as Sean called out to her, 'How about a roadie, Alice?'

'Roadie?' she said, confused and shaking her head.

'Before you head back to Charleville.'

'No, I'm staying here tonight,' she said. 'But thank you anyway, Sean.'

'Come and have a drink with me? I'm about to take a break for a couple of hours.'

Alice shook her head and forced a smile. 'Thank you, Sean. I've got some work to do. I'm actually here working.'

'I thought you were having a date with Billy Burke and that you two had a blue. He didn't look terribly happy when he left. You're certainly not doing handstands. I was going to offer a shoulder to cry on.' He looked hopeful.

'Business,' she said, shaking her head. 'We were just catching up on some business.'

He shrugged and looked at her, but she knew he didn't believe what she was saying. 'You sure I can't talk you into a drink?'

Alice hesitated for a moment. She had known Sean in the early years of high school, and he was a good person, but there was no point in giving him any encouragement. She didn't want

148

to go out with him. The only person she wanted to go out with was someone who could perhaps lead to a long-term relationship, and Sean Barlow certainly wasn't the sort of man she was interested in making that life with, no matter what a good guy he was.

'Thanks anyway, Sean, but I've got some work to do. I'll see you later.' With that, she turned and walked through the door and up the steps to the room she'd booked on the first floor.

CHAPTER 20

Callie Cartwright tried to organise a craft afternoon on Saturday. But with late notice, Sophie and Alice were the only committee members free to attend.

'Even though it's only the three of us, we're still going to have it,' Callie said when she called Alice to confirm on Friday night. 'Stay for dinner; we're having a bit of a barbeque.'

'Are you sure?'

'Yes, and bring an overnight bag and stay the night.'

Alice thought about it and considered the number of nights she spent home alone in her flat. 'Thank you, Callie. I'll accept; that sounds lovely. I've been talking to Tilly and Bec, and they tell me that I need to get out, so an afternoon and evening at *Kilcoy Station* would fit the bill. What can I bring?'

'Just bring yourself and your craft stuff. I've got a sewing room out on the verandah. Braden's first wife was really into crafts and used to spend a lot of time there, apparently. I've never used it because I'm not crafty.'

'You're happy to have it at your place with

your hands full with the kids?'

'Of course. We can get a lot done, even with just the three of us.'

Alice drove into *Kilcoy Station* after lunch on Saturday afternoon. It was the first time she'd been to the Cartwright's station. Her eyes widened as she drove through the gate and looked at the almost manicured paddocks full of healthy-looking cattle. It was very different to the property she'd sold after her parents passed away.

As she drove down the long driveway, a red brick house was ahead, with a huge shed to the side and a few cars parked outside.

As she drove in, she spotted some kids playing football and realised one was Beau, her refugee. She hoped that Billy Burke wouldn't be there, too.

She left her overnight bag in the back of the car until she figured out what the night was going to be like and whether she would stay or not. She carried in her handbag a soft bag of craft fabric, and the pavlova she'd whipped up last night. Even though Callie said not to bring anything, Alice knew dessert always went down well.

The boys ignored her until she walked to the

gate at the front of the long, wide house. She didn't know the Cartwright boys, but it was definitely young Beau. Alice was pleased to see his hair was clean and shiny, and even though his clothes were old jeans and a T-shirt, he looked clean. He stood there watching her for a moment, then smiled and ran over.

'Hello,' he said.

'Hello, Beau, how are you?'

'I'm really good, thank you.'

'It's good to see you looking a bit happier,' Alice said.

You look really different,' he said. 'You look like a girl now.'

Alice laughed. 'What did I look like before?'

'You looked like someone who was in a job.'

'Funny that,' she said. 'I was doing my job that day.'

'What are you doing here? Have you come to work with the cattle like Billy?'

Her breath caught. The worst thing that could happen would be Billy Burke being out here, too.

'No, I've come to help Mrs Cartwright and Mrs...' She paused to think of Sophie's last name. 'Mrs Mason with some stuff for the ball.'

'Can kids come to this ball?' he asked. 'Rory and Nigel were telling me about it. They really hope that kids can come.'

'I'm not sure,' Alice said. 'But probably, seeing it's a fundraiser. The more, the better.'

'What's a fundraiser?' he asked.

'When we ask people to pay to come and have a good time, and then the money goes to someone who needs it.'

'Like poor people?' His eyes were hopeful, and she wondered what sort of situation he and Billy actually lived in.

'No, more like group stuff. We're talking about the aged care facility, the new youth centre, and things like that.'

'A new youth centre, like the one you took me to down in Charleville? Where you fed me, and where I played on the computer for an hour before you drove me home? I meant to say thank you for rescuing me. I was pretty naughty to do that, and Billy made it clear that it won't be happening again. I'll be in bigger trouble if I do that again.'

'What happened?' she asked, curious, hoping he hadn't had a hiding or anything like that. It was unfair to ask him because she wasn't here in a work capacity, but he looked happy and clean, so hopefully, her talk with Billy had worked.

'No football watching on television for two weeks,' he said, his eyes downcast.

'And that's hard for you?'

'Oh yes,' he said. 'I'm not even allowed to know the results until Monday. He's so mean. He makes me stay in my room, and he watches it with the volume down so I can't hear it. He even took my phone off me so I couldn't watch it.'

'And what did you learn from that?' Alice said as they walked through the gate together.

'Well, I learned if you do the wrong thing, there are consequences, and the consequences usually take away something you really like. You have to spend that time thinking.'

'Sounds like it's been a good lesson for you then, Beau.'

'It has. I'm sorry I did it, but I'm not sorry I met you. You were very nice to me.'

'That's my job.'

'Yeah, it might be a job, but I think you're a nice person too. And looking like a girl makes you look friendlier. Do you play footy?'

'I used to play footy when I was at school.'

'Do you wanna come play with us?'

Alice chuckled. 'I'll take you up on that another time, but at the moment, the ladies are in the sewing room waiting for me. We've got some jobs to do. Good to see you, Beau, and good to see you looking so happy.'

With a wide, cheeky grin, he turned and ran back to join the Cartwright boys. Soon, there were shouts of 'faster, faster' coming from the paddock as she walked to the breezeway and knocked on the back door.

Callie came to the door with one of the twins on her hip.

'Hi, Callie.'

'Hi, Alice, I'm so glad you're here early. I'm sorry I didn't hear your car come in. I'm having a drama with the kids.'

'A drama?'

'Yeah, they ate something they shouldn't, and we've got the resultant nappy mess,' Callie said. 'Munro is all clean. Can you nurse him for me? Sophie is dealing with the other one while I'm cleaning up the mess.'

'Yep, I can hold him. But I'm not used to nursing babies.'

'You'll be fine. Head up the hall with him to

the last door on the right. We'll meet you there shortly.'

Alice walked up the hallway with the unfamiliar heavy bundle in her arms. She couldn't remember the last time she'd held a child. In fact, she wondered if she ever had held a baby. Munro reached up and grabbed one of Alice's blonde curls, tugging at it. His fingers headed for his mouth.

'Oh no, you don't, little one,' she said. 'You don't want a mouthful of shampoo and conditioner.'

She freed the hair from the little boy's chubby fingers and smiled down at him.

'More, more,' the little boy said.

'More hair or more food?'

'More yum,' the little boy said, patting Alice on the face with those beautiful fat fingers.

'You're a sweetie, aren't you?' she said.

'Mum, mum, mum, mum.'

'No, I'm not your mum, as you well know.'

She reached the last door at the end of the wooden floor hallway, her eyes wide. The room was full of sunshine, with three sewing machines set up along a bench in the shade. Sunlight poured through windows that ran the whole length of the front wall. She stood there, looking out over the vista of paddocks stretching as far as she could see, and in the far distance, blue mountains rose on the horizon. It had been such a good season of rain; everything was lush and green, and it was a beautiful view to look at.

She wondered how much land Callie and Braden worked and how they managed. It was a long way out of town, but it reminded her of growing up in her parents' place. She swore she would never go back to the land, but now that she had time to think it over, she realised it was because those last few months with her dad not well and the property being rundown had tainted her view.

She'd loved growing up on the farm, the animals, and the wide open spaces. There was no comparison to the small flat where she lived, spending most of her nights alone watching television.

Emotion lodged in her throat as she looked down at the little boy. 'You're just gorgeous, aren't you? If only my life had turned out differently. If only I had met somebody and could have a child like you.'

But it looked like that wasn't going to

happen. In the corner was a playpen she hadn't noticed before, with another baby girl sitting there playing with some blocks. Alice carried Munro over and carefully put him in with the little girl. 'I suppose it's okay for you just to sit in here together. You must be Sophie's. Are you Ruby Rose?'

The little girl looked up and smiled, greeting her with two front teeth. 'Well, you're a beautiful girl too.'

She walked back to the window as the two babies settled in and started playing with the blocks again. She was pensive as she stared out the window. She really had to do something. She loved her job and living in this area; she just needed a better personal life to complete it.

She stared out the window, thinking about how much money she had saved and how Bec had agreed that she could come out and run the youth centre here at Augathella. It was time to try and find a place of her own, but if the truth be known, she'd prefer something with a bit of land. She'd have to think carefully about what she was going to buy. Her job was secure now that there was government funding as well as additional seed funding from Chloe's group, so she could afford a mortgage. She just had to work out how much she could afford to spend. Maybe a little house that she could do up on a couple of acres, not too far from town, so she didn't have too far to drive to work.

She jumped as someone spoke behind her.

'Penny for your thoughts,' Sophie said.

'Yeah, I was just looking out at this beautiful view. I didn't realise how much I missed being on the land.'

'You grew up out at Allenvale, didn't you?'

'Yeah, when Mum and Dad passed away, and the farm was sold, there wasn't much left. I had to sell it to pay the mortgage because, at that stage, I couldn't afford it. It took me a while to save up to go to uni.'

'There's no doubt about you being a worker. And I hope you know how much you're appreciated too. We're all really excited that you're coming to town to run the Choice for Youth branch here. So are the kids.'

'The kids don't know me.'

'They know they'll love you. And I've heard you're pretty good. Apparently, Billy's boy has been singing your praises.'

'Young Beau?' Alice chuckled.

'Yep, you made a hit with him when you rescued him from Charleville.'

'He's a good kid. I want to make sure he gets cared for properly.'

'I'm sure Billy cares for him. It's a difficult situation, I believe.'

'I really can't talk about it. I suppose it's gossiping, but it's also my job. Let's say he looks great today, happy, clean, and not so scrawny.'

'You remember Kent when he was growing up?' Sophie picked up her daughter and cuddled her. 'Oh, that's right, you were a couple of years ahead of us.'

'Yep, and when you're in primary school, you don't take much notice of the younger kids. Why? What was it with Kent?'

'Kent was a string bean, would you believe it? Even when we started going out when he was sixteen, he was skinny as, and look at him now.'

Alice called the tall, strong man to mind. 'Well, you'd never know that. He's certainly a big man.'

'We can't judge poor little Beau by his size. He probably eats like a horse and burns it all up.'

Alice chuckled again. 'He wanted me to come and play football with him.'

'No football for you today; we've got some masks to make,' Sophie said.

At the last ball meeting, they decided to move away from the Australian animal theme for the adults and go with colourful masks. Sophie, Alice, and Callie had volunteered to do some sewing. They were going to sell the masks at a stall in town, and Alice had even suggested they do an online shop for those who wanted to order privately. They were making eye masks and full face masks, with a pattern from the internet and all the fabric bought. Today was the day to start putting some together.

Callie walked in the door, holding another baby. 'Alice, this is Miss Meggie, the mistress of disgusting nappies, but she's all clean now.' She dropped a kiss on her head and walked over to the playpen, putting the little girl in with the two other babies. 'Now, you three behave for a while.'

She might as well not have spoken because they were all engrossed in crawling around and playing with the toys.

'So, are we ready to work?' Alice asked.

'We are,' Callie replied.

CHAPTER 21

By the end of the afternoon, seven masks had been completed. Sophie had made four, Alice had made two, and Callie, between getting up and looking after the kids, the twins, and getting food for the four boys every time they came in saying they were hungry, had managed to complete one. The chatter and laughter had filled the room as they worked, and Alice felt absolutely content. It had been a long time since she spent time with friends like this, and she felt welcomed into their friendship.

The children had been well-behaved, and Alice had found herself helping Callie a couple of times, nursing the children, and actually giving Munro a bottle. She nursed him, sitting in the chair in the corner of the room in the sunshine, as he chugged down a bottle of milk in about two minutes flat. His wide eyes looked up at her. He burped when he finished the bottle, pulled it out of his mouth, and threw it on the floor. 'More.'

'No, young man, you've had one. That's plenty. I'll get you a rusk to chew on.'

'More bottle,' Munro said.

'He's gorgeous, isn't he?' Sophie said. 'He's a little character.'

'I think he's got the energy and the character of the three other boys combined,' Callie said. 'He watches them like a hawk, and you can see he's itching to get out there and play with them, whereas Meggie is the quiet one,' Callie said. 'She sits back and observes. It's going to be interesting watching them grow up.'

'I honestly don't know how you do it, Callie. You've got the three boys, you work, you've got the twins, and now you're having another one. You must have so much energy. You make me feel guilty. I'm exhausted when I get home from a day at the centre. I crash in front of the TV. From now on, I'll be making masks every night.'

'Do you like living by yourself, Alice?' Sophie asked.

Alice thought for a moment and looked up. 'No, I don't. Actually, I've been thinking a lot about it lately. Tilly Tingle is trying to talk me into going on one of those online things, you know, Tinder and those apps.'

'Why on earth would a lovely-looking girl like you need to do that?' Callie asked.

'Picking's pretty slim in the district,' she said.

'Do you ever go out to meet guys?' Sophie asked.

Alice shook her head. 'Not really.'

'So you think you're going to meet someone sitting in your flat all night watching TV? And you work with kids from twelve to eighteen all day.'

Alice nodded. 'I suppose.'

'Well, I think we need to create some social occasions for you. Tonight is the start,' Callie said.

'The start?' Alice chuckled.

'We're going to find you a fella,' Sophie said.

'A fella?' Alice burst out laughing.

'An Augathella fella,' Callie said with a giggle.

'I'm actually moving to Augathella,' Alice said. She was having fun with these girls.

'Really?' Callie said. 'That's great. You can come around a lot more.'

'And you can come out to our place too,' Sophie said.

'Oh, girls, thank you so much. You've made

me feel so welcome.'

'We enjoy your company, Alice.'

'So, tonight, who's coming?' Sophie asked.

Callie said, 'Well, it's all of us, including Kent, of course, and Alan Humphreys.'

'Who's Alan Humphreys?' Alice asked. 'I haven't heard of him.'

'He bought the property on the town side of Jon's, and he's working with the guys today,' Callie said.

'Is he young?' Alice asked.

Sophie and Callie looked at each other. 'Depends what you call young,' Callie said with a cheeky grin.

'Less than forty?' Alice ventured.

'He won't suit. I think he's on the wrong side of sixty. He owns a few properties around the region, and he's only here working to get this one off the ground. He's going to put a manager in. Nice house on it, though.'

'The man's more important than the house,' Alice said.

'And he brought a couple of his stockmen with him. I don't know them, but they'll be staying for the barbeque as well. A couple of young blokes, but I think they are pretty young, as in their early twenties from what I saw when they arrived with him before in his truck this morning,' Callie added.

'Billy's coming,' Sophie said.

'Billy Burke?' Alice said, her heart sinking.

'Billy's older than the other young guys, Sophie, but he's still not what you'd call old.' Callie said.

'True,' Alice agreed.

'That's right. You were involved the day Beau skipped school and ended up out here a couple of weeks ago,' Callie nodded. 'Billy's a nice guy.'

Alice didn't comment.

Callie glanced across at her. 'What do you think, Alice?'

'No cattleman for me. When I get married and have kids, I'll be choosing a professional man. No offence to you girls; I know you both married property owners, but I want someone who goes off to work in a suit and tie, carrying a briefcase.'

Callie and Sophie looked at each other with a frown.

'Why would you want someone stuffy like that?' Sophie asked.

'Security of a profession, I guess,' Alice said.

Sophie placed another finished mask on the table. 'Nothing to do with security, Alice. It's all about love.'

Callie nodded. 'That's right. It's not the *security* of a profession, sweetie. It's how hard a person works. Life on the land is not easy, as I'm sure you know.'

'Yeah, I guess what formed my opinions and my needs was watching my dad lose everything we had,' Alice said.

'How long ago was that?' Callie asked.

'Back in the drought.'

Sophie nodded. 'They were tough times, but we all got through it. We've restocked now, the rains are great, and the property is going well. You don't need a man to go off in a suit carrying a briefcase to provide security. You need a good man with good, solid working ideals. A man who loves you. Doesn't matter what he does.'

'Anyway, come on, girls, enough of that. I'm going to go and put these two down for a sleep,' Callie said. 'What about Ruby Rose?'

'Yeah, Ruby can go down too. I brought the porta-cot.'

'Then we'll start getting this barbeque sorted. You are going to stay the night, aren't you, Alice?' Callie asked.

Alice thought long and hard. Callie had been so welcoming; it would seem churlish to say no, even though the thought of socialising with Billy Burke didn't appeal.

'Of course, I am, as long as it's all right with you. I brought an overnight bag.'

'Great,' Callie said. 'Come on, girls, let's go party.'

CHAPTER 22

Callie showed Alice her room on the other side of a breezeway, which appeared to divide the large house into two separate wings.

Braden was setting up a barbeque outside of the breezeway space, and the boys were running around. Alice was interested to see that Beau was still here with the Cartwright boys, but there was no sign of Billy. Their meeting had ended on an "agree to disagree" note, and she was disappointed that he was going to be there tonight because she would find it very hard to relax when he turned up.

The problem was that not only did she disagree with his attitude and his brusqueness, but aside from that, she was very interested in him. She wondered what made him tick. At times when they'd been speaking over the table in the pub bistro about the various concerns that she had about Beau, she had found it hard to look away as her eyes roved over his face, noting the strength not only in his physical build but the steadfastness and strength with which he held and expressed his views.

She tried to explain to him carefully, without getting him offside or cross, that having responsibility for a twelve-year-old boy involved a lot more than keeping him clean and fed. Although they both agreed that it wasn't his fault that Billy refused to shower, she suggested that perhaps he should see a child psychologist to deal with his stubbornness.

Alice shrugged as Callie shut the door behind her. She put her bag on the bed, unzipped it, and pulled out the summer dress she had packed, followed by the soft pink cashmere cardigan she'd bought in Charleville a couple of weeks ago. Spring was just around the corner, and the weather was balmy. Maybe she should have worn jeans and a T-shirt tonight, but she wanted to dress well because you never know who you'll meet at a big gathering like the Cartwrights were obviously having tonight. Anything was better than going on that online dating thing in a town like this. It would only take one person to see her on there, and the likelihood of that was very high; she'd be a laughingstock.

'What if Gladys got a hold of it?' she thought, imagining what she'd say. Although her friend Beryl had been pulling Gladys into line lately, Beryl had actually stood up and criticised one of Gladys's statements at the meeting last week.

Gladys had flushed, sat down, and busied herself with her sewing, not daring to chip back at Beryl as she was wont to do.

Alice shook her dress and hung it on the hanger that Callie had taken out of the wardrobe for her. She quickly went into the bathroom, washed her face, brushed her hair, and put on a tiny bit of makeup. It was a casual barbeque, but she didn't want to look too dressed down.

A few minutes later, she strapped on her pink sandals, fluffed up her hair one more time with her fingers, and opened the door. She walked down the hall, hearing the sound of voices growing louder as she got closer to the breezeway. She was nervous stepping out there by herself. Eventually, she lifted her pace and stood at the door, looking out into the wide space. The sun was low in the sky, the lights were still not on, and the boys were still running around, playing with the dogs and making lots of noise. She smiled. She wanted Beau to just be one of the kids. If she was right, he looked a little bit cleaner today. His hair was shining in the late afternoon light, and although his shirt was untucked, he looked cleaner than he had the last two times she'd seen him.

She jumped as a voice came from behind her. 'Satisfied, Miss Templeton?'

She turned slowly, the fragrance of subtle aftershave filling her senses. She looked up into Billy Burke's blue eyes but could not read his expression.

'Satisfied?' she asked her smile tight. 'Satisfied with what?'

'You were watching Beau very intently,' he said.

'I was watching the boys play, smiling when I saw what a fun time they were having.' There was no way on God's earth she was going to say she'd been looking at Beau's hair and clothes. 'And it's the weekend, Mr Burke. I'm not working.'

'So, have you made your decision about a notification yet?'

She had, but she wasn't going to tell him that. 'As I said, Mr Burke, it's the weekend. If you want to have a meeting with me, arrange a time for next week.'

'Oh, for God's sake,' he said. 'Surely you can give me a simple yes or no. Put me out of my misery, woman.'

'Woman?' she said, her eyebrows arching. 'Isn't that a bit disrespectful?'

'Isn't keeping me hanging disrespectful? Two-way street, Miss Templeton.'

Billy drained the can of beer he was holding, crushed it, and turned away to put it in the bin nearby with the other cans.

Alice waited for him to return and finish the conversation, but her mouth dropped open when he walked outside without looking back at her.

'How rude!' she said under her breath.

She stood there for a moment, seriously considering putting her drink on the table, going up to get her bag, sneaking out the back door, and leaving. Billy Burke had unsettled her; she didn't want to spend another moment in his company, and if he spoke to her like that again, she *would* leave.

As she stood there, debating what to do, Braden approached her, accompanied by an older, short, stocky man.

'Alice, have you met Alan Humphreys yet?' he asked.

'Hello, Braden. No, I haven't.' She turned and smiled at the newcomer, who was obviously the new property owner next door to Fallon and Jon's house the girls had been talking about

'Hello, Alan.' She smiled and took the hand that was offered

'Nice to meet you, Alice. I hear you're moving back to the district.'

She raised her eyebrows. 'Things certainly get around quickly.'

Braden apologised, 'I'm sorry if I spoke out of turn, but Cal told me you're moving back to Augathella to run the local branch of Choice for Youth up here. I thought you might be looking for somewhere to live.

'No, that's fine, Braden, and yes, I am.'

'I told Braden I'm looking for someone to move into my farmhouse,' Alan said. 'Braden said you may be interested.'

'There's not a lot of accommodation in town with all the new families that have moved into the district recently,' Braden said.

'Yes, that's one of the factors that got Bec's application approved for a local branch of CFY for the town.' She turned to Alan, her eyes wide. 'A farmhouse? How far out of town? Do you have more than one house on the property?'

Alan chuckled. 'I do, but my home is down at Narrabri in New South Wales. I bought this one, and I will eventually put a manager in, but at the moment, we're not running much stock, so it will run itself until I find a suitable manager. It's next door to the Ingram's property, not too far out of town. Do you know where they live?'

'I do.' Alice nodded as excitement began to build. She'd been worried about finding somewhere to live and certainly didn't want to drive up from Charleville every day.

The older man scratched his head and frowned. 'I'm not happy about leaving the house empty. I've heard about squatters moving around the state. It's happened a bit in our district, and I was hoping that someone would move in and rent it from me. A very reasonable rent,' he added.

Alice considered his words and nodded slowly. 'Thank you, Mr Humphreys. I'll certainly give it some thought.'

'It'd be an informal arrangement,' he said. 'No lease or anything like that.'

'And how long do you think it would be before you need to move a manager in?'

He shrugged. 'I'm not sure yet, but do have a think about it, won't you?'

Alice nodded again. 'Yes, I will.'

'Thanks.' Alan walked away and headed to the drinks fridge, which had been opened quite frequently over the last ten minutes.

'I'm sorry, Alice. I hope I didn't put you in an awkward situation,' Braden apologised again.

'No, it's okay, Braden, not at all.' She wasn't going to mention Billy Burke, but she glanced over at him. She drew in a quick breath, and her face heated as she realised he was watching her.

Braden's eyes narrowed, and when he turned to see who had made her blush, Billy Burke was leaning against the side wall at the end of the breezeway, watching the boys play football.

'Are you okay?' he asked.

'Yes, I'm fine, Braden. Thanks for inviting me and for the introduction to Mr Humphreys.'

'Our pleasure. It'll be a good night. We've still got a few more coming—a few young ones closer to your age.' Braden glanced at her almost empty glass. 'Can I get you another drink?' Braden asked.

Alice made a quick decision. She avoided looking at Billy Burke and nodded at Braden.

'Yes, please. Another wine would be good. Thank you.'

***

Billy knew he'd had those two beers too quickly, but he was trying to calm himself down. It didn't matter how much he drank as long as he stayed fairly sober because Braden had offered him a place for his swag behind the big shed. It made sense because Beau was staying the night with Rory Cartwright, and it meant that Billy didn't have to drive out again tomorrow to pick him up. They could both stay the night and go home mid-morning. He was sure Braden could find him some jobs to help out with around the property. It was the least he could do to thank the Cartwights for the way they had welcomed Beau—and him—to their home.

His eyes narrowed as he watched Alan Humphreys talking to Alice. Alan took a step closer to her. Billy felt sick when she smiled at Alan so enthusiastically.

'What are you up to, you old bugger?' he muttered to himself. He turned his back and lifted his beer to take a sip, then remembered the can was empty. It was none of his business what Alan said to her. Alice Templeton was none of his business at all. The only thing he had to worry about was whether she was going to do that stupid notification or not.

He knew he could take care of Beau just fine, and he shouldn't have to prove himself until he'd done something really bad. At least he'd gotten Beau in the shower tonight and put a clean shirt on him. The promise of playing football all night and tomorrow morning had spurred Beau on, and he'd agreed with everything Billy suggested. Not only that, Beau had chatted non-stop all the way from their place out to *Kilcoy Station*, his happiness giving Billy a warm and fuzzy feeling in his chest.

He shook himself mentally. 'A warm and fuzzy feeling in my chest? For God's sake!' he thought.

CHAPTER 23

Alice thoroughly enjoyed the night. It didn't take long to settle in and feel comfortable with the group of people, although she studiously ignored Billy Burke. He was the one who made her feel uncomfortable. She laughed and chatted with Sophie and Callie, and they couldn't resist making more plans for the upcoming ball.

At the end of the night, it was a typical Australian barbeque. The women headed to the kitchen to put away the leftover food. Alice helped Fallon load the dishwasher while Callie went to settle the twins, who had woken up for a bottle.

To his credit, Fallon's husband, Jon, helped them carry some dishes, and Braden came in and offered to help wash up the trays.

Fallon shooed him out, saying, 'Go and chat to the men.'

Alice looked at Fallon curiously after Braden went outside.

Fallon smiled at her. 'The guys work hard out on the property, and I know even at smoko they don't get much of a chance to yarn.'

Jon chuckled. 'We're usually talking about cattle issues, fertilisers, and feed.'

'Sweetie, you go out with the guys too,' Fallon said to her husband. 'We can finish off here.'

'Did you enjoy yourself tonight, Alice?' Fallon ran hot water into the sink, and Alice picked up a tea towel

'I did,' she said. 'It was good to meet new people.'

Fallon glanced at Alice. 'Billy Burke seems like a nice guy.'

Alice shrugged. 'I didn't speak to him much.' She certainly wasn't going to mention her professional encounter with him.

'Yes, and young Beau has really bonded with our boys,' Callie said. 'It's good to see. I think he may have had a bit of a difficult background.'

Again, Alice didn't comment.

'Anyway, he's settled in, and they've organised a sleepover for the weekend after next. They're all football mad.'

'Good exercise, and good to see them out playing around in the fresh air,' Alice said. 'Too many kids these days come into the centre, and

180

all they want to do is put their heads in front of a computer and play games.'

'We're pretty strict about that,' Callie said, 'although they are allowed to play a little—a few hours a week.'

The last of the benches were wiped down, and the dishwasher was whirring away in the background. Jon had gone back out to the fire to chat with the men, and Fallon yawned.

'I think I'll go out and get Jon moving,' she said. 'It'll be another hour or two, and then Ryan will wake up. I might feed him before we go, and then he'll sleep all the way home. With a bit of luck, he'll stay asleep when we get there.'

Callie nodded. 'Yes, the twins have gone down for the count now.'

'Enjoy your freedom, Alice,' Callie said. 'One day you'll be like this. Your whole life will revolve around sleep time, nappies, washing, and food.'

'Sounds wonderful to me,' Alice said. 'I can't wait for that time of my life.'

Fallon shook her head. 'Don't wish your life away, love.'

'Fallon, if you're heading off, I'll see you at the next meeting.' Sophie and Kent had left earlier as Ruby Rose was being a little bit fractious.

Callie walked over to Alice. 'Alice, would you like to sit and have a cup of coffee with me?'

Alice shook her head. 'No, Callie, you head off to bed, and I'll head off. Thanks so much for offering me a bed for the night. I really appreciate it. I don't think I would've enjoyed driving back to town in the dark.'

'No, you were able to relax, have a wine or two, and then head off after breakfast in the morning. Make sure you stay, too, because, on Sunday mornings, Braden does a big cook-up—pancakes and everything for the boys. It's the highlight of their week. "Anything better than wheat?" Nigel always says.'

'Thank you, that sounds lovely, but I'll see how I go. We'll see what time I wake up.'

Fallon came over and hugged Alice. 'It's been good to spend some time with you, Alice. I'll see you soon.' She headed up the hallway to get her baby out of the back bedroom.

'Callie, you look exhausted,' Alice said. 'I'll make my way up to my room. I might even go out and grab some fresh air before I go to bed. The stars are magnificent out here. That's about the only thing I miss about being on the land.'

'Okay, Alice, thank you. You sleep well. If you get cold, there's a spare blanket in the wardrobe in that bedroom.'

'I'm fine, thank you.'

'And there should be soap and shampoo in the bathroom.'

Alice loved Callie; she was so kind and welcoming. 'I'm fine. You go and get some sleep, and I'll see you in the morning. If I wake up early, I'll help Braden in the kitchen.'

'Night, Alice. It's been lovely to have you here. I'll see you in the morning.'

Alice took one last look around the kitchen. After the two women had gone and everything was in place, she opened the door that led out to the breezeway and glanced across to the right. There were still three or four men around the fire. The older boys had gone to bed about ten-thirty when Braden had herded them inside.

She was surprised to see Billy Burke still there. Perhaps Beau was staying the night, and he was going to drive home anyway. She shrugged, but instead of going out into the wing of the house, she turned left and took a door she had noticed before, leading to the other side of the yard.

It was a beautiful night, slightly cool but with a promise of spring in the air, which made her think of the ball. They still had so much to do, and the spring ball was only about four weeks away.

After breakfast, she would head back to her hotel room. She had brought her sewing machine from Charleville.

Hopefully, the house out at Alan Humphreys' would be suitable. It would be much better than driving to and from Charleville until she found somewhere to live.

The night was clear, and a beautiful patchwork of brilliant stars covered the sky. In the east, the horizon brightened as the moon rose.

Alice walked over to the fence on the other side of the big shed, climbed up on the bottom rung, and rested her chin on her hands, looking up as the universe swelled around her. She felt insignificant under the vast sky.

The only sounds were the occasional lowing from the cattle in a nearby paddock and the soft rustling of something in the long grass over the fence.

Peace and serenity enveloped her, and she

took a deep breath, enjoying the beautiful evening.

She stood there for about fifteen minutes, watching the sky, and then a slight breeze puffed in. She rubbed her arms, jumped down, and pulled her cardigan more tightly around her.

As she turned to go back to the house, she noticed the glow of a cigarette between her and the door to the breezeway, and she hesitated. Perhaps it was Braden. Maybe the other men had gone. She really didn't feel like talking to anyone. She was feeling calm and at ease, and, to be honest, her main fear was that it would be Billy Burke. She certainly didn't want to get into another conversation with him when she was feeling so mellow.

She strolled back toward the door at the back of the breezeway.

'Don't worry, Alice. It's only me.'

'I'm sorry, I didn't know there was anybody out here.'

It *was* Billy Burke.

As she approached, he dropped his cigarette to the ground, twisted his boot on it, then reached down, picked it up, and put it in his pocket.

'That's okay,' she said. 'I wasn't—'

'Couldn't sleep?' he asked.

'No, I just came out to have a few minutes and look at the sky. It's certainly a beautiful night.' She couldn't believe they were having a normal conversation.

'It certainly is,' he agreed.

'What about you? Are you staying the night?' she asked.

'I normally go home, but Beau was pretty keen to stay with the boys, and apparently, there's a promise of a big cook-up for breakfast from Braden. Beau twisted my arm.'

'It's good of you to take that into consideration,' she said.

'He's had a tough time, Alice. It's the least I can do.' He patted his pocket. 'To be honest, it does my head in. I don't usually smoke, but standing out here tonight, watching the interaction of the kids, I realise how much Beau has missed out on over the past few months.'

Alice nodded. 'He did seem to be having a good time. I watched them for a while, too.'

The usual tension between them seemed to have disappeared, and Alice relaxed.

'Do you think you'll stay in the locality long?' she asked.

'To be honest,' Billy replied, 'I don't know. My job is itinerant, and I follow the work, but seeing how Beau has settled since he hooked up with the Cartwright boys and how he's also settled a little more in school, I'm starting to think that I might have to settle here for a while.'

'Is there a lot of work?' she asked.

He nodded. 'I think there are enough properties around, depending on what time of year it is. I should get enough. If not, I can always resort to truck driving or working in a rural store.'

'But what about Beau?'

'No, I'd only do short trips. I'd make sure I was doing a run that was only between local towns. I did some truck driving for a while.'

'You obviously like working on the land,' she said.

'I love being outside,' he said. 'I couldn't think of anything worse than being stuck in a building or an office all day.'

Alice shrugged. 'I suppose it all boils down to what you're doing and whether you're doing something that you love.'

'Do you enjoy your job?' he asked.

'I do. I've been doing it for a while.'

'And you've always lived around here?'

She shook her head. 'No, I've travelled overseas. I lived in Brisbane for a while.'

'Why Augathella?' he asked curiously.

'I guess it's where my heart is. I always say that where you spend your formative years always tugs you back. What about you? Where did you come from?

'Mount Isa.'

'And you've got no desire to go back to where you grew up?'

'I certainly haven't. There are not very good memories back there.'

He continued speaking but seemed embarrassed. 'Not that I'm whingeing, and don't worry, I don't want to lay my problems on you, but it was tough.'

He talked about Mary and Beau and moving to the Northern Territory.

Alice was surprised by how talkative Billy was; it was as though a different man was talking to her than the Billy Burke she'd known so far.

'Did you always work on the land?' she asked.

'I worked in the mines when I first left uni. Talk about not being in a building—I was underground a lot of the time.'

'Uni?' Alice felt awful for having made a stereotypical judgment.

'Yeah, I did Agriculture as soon as I left school. A few things happened, and I couldn't stay there anymore, so I went to the Northern Territory and started working with cattle. I found what I really love to do.'

'I think that's the life if you can find contentment in what you do every day,' Alice said.

'It is. I was going well until I suddenly had to take care of Beau. Life's been a bit tough since then.' He cleared his throat. 'I need to apologise. I think I've been pretty rude to you, Alice.'

'No, not at all, don't worry,' she said, meaning it. 'I probably wasn't as polite to you as I should've been either, Billy. I'm sorry.'

In the growing light from the rising moon, she saw a flash of a smile. He held out his hand. 'Start again?'

His hand was rough, warm, and strong, and Alice was taken aback as a tingle ran up her arm to her shoulder and a warm feeling fluttered in her stomach.

'A new start sounds good,' she said, clearing

her throat and looking down. 'Anyway, I'd better get to bed. It's been nice chatting with you, Billy.'

'And you too, Alice.'

She turned and hurried for the door, knowing that he was watching her.

CHAPTER 24

'Uncle Billy, wake up, wake up!'

Billy sat up quickly in his swag. 'Beau, what's wrong? Is that you?'

'It is. Can I go riding on horses with Rory and Nigel before breakfast?'

'Riding on horses? You mean—hang on, stay there, don't go away.' He reached out for his jeans, slipped them on, climbed out of the swag, and clipped his belt. He stretched, then rubbed his hands through his hair.

Beau, Rory, and Nigel were standing at the other end of his swag.

'So, okay, tell me what's happening,' Billy said.

Rory stepped forward. 'Nigel and I just go for a ride down to the dam in the morning to give our horses a run, and the dogs come with us. We just wondered; we really hoped that Beau could come for a ride with us.'

'How long since you've ridden, Beau?'

'Uncle Billy! You always forget. I used to ride all the time at home, remember?'

Billy smothered a grin. When Beau used "Uncle," it was usually to get his own way.

Billy nodded. 'I do, mate, but it's been a while. You reckon you'll be okay?'

'It's okay, Mr Burke,' Nigel said. 'We've got a really quiet pony—'

Beau cut in with an expression of disgust. 'I don't need a quiet pony, Nigel!'

'Anyway, Dad's in the shed; he'll sort us out,' Rory said.

'Can I please go, Uncle Billy? Please, please, please,' Beau pleaded.

'I can't see a problem with that. Be careful, mate.' He reached over and rubbed the top of Beau's head. For the first time, Beau didn't flinch or pull away.

Billy knew how much he owed the Cartwrights. He stood there, the morning chill cool on his bare chest and back.

As he watched the boys run back to the shed, Billy looked around. He had set his swag up between the shed and the fence line of the main paddock. He looked down at his swag and then across to the trough with the tap on the back wall and decided to wash there. Braden had offered him the use of the shed bathroom, but he only needed to use the toilet there; he'd wash outside.

When he left the shed, he walked over, ran

192

the tap, cupped his hands under the cool water, rubbed it over his face, and ran his wet fingers through his hair.

As he turned to walk back across to his swag, ready to put his shirt on and pack it up, his eyes widened as Alice walked around the back of the shed.

She stopped suddenly, and he was pleased to see the colour rising on her face.

When they shook hands last night, he'd been quite taken aback by the zing her fingers had raised on his skin, and he could tell now from the colour on her face that she wasn't immune to him.

'I'm sorry,' she said. 'I didn't realise you were around here. I was going for a walk before breakfast.'

'Not worried at all. Would you like some company?'

'No, no.' She shook her head. 'It's okay, you go and do whatever you're doing, and I'll... I'll go the other way.'

Billy grinned as he watched her retreat.

CHAPTER 25

The following week raced by as Alice drove from Augathella to Charleville every second day. On Tuesday, she met Alan Humphreys at his house and was pleased to see that it was a nice place to live and that he was keen to let her move in. The rent they agreed on was very reasonable, but he did tell her that there was some stock down the back if she heard noises at night.

'It's okay, Alan,' she said. 'I spent a lot of my childhood and teenage years out on a property. I can look after myself.'

They shook on the deal before she headed back to Charleville that evening, and as soon as Alice got home, she packed up her gear, ready to bring it up in the car the following day. For the last couple of years, she had travelled a lot and lived in small apartments. The only thing that went everywhere with her was her sewing machine, so it didn't take too long to pack everything up. Alan was to leave late last night to head back to his property in New South Wales, so she decided to go by the property this morning and unpack her gear before she went into the youth centre.

The sky was heavy, and the weather had succumbed to a low-pressure system over the weekend, threatening to bring a lot of rain. She thought about the weather and the floods as she drove onto the property. That was one downside: If it flooded, she'd get cut off out here. She'd noticed a couple of creeks on the way out, but there were no cars or trucks to be seen.

She let herself in, looked around, and was very satisfied with where she would be living. From what Alan said last night, he was hoping to have a manager lined up, but they weren't going to start for another six weeks at least, so it looked like she'd have plenty of time to find somewhere permanent to live in town.

Alice had looked at her investment account last night and thought maybe she could soon afford to buy herself some land. A small holding, just to have some space. Maybe on the edge of town. She decided to see the local agent to check what was available and see if she could purchase something and have it settled by the time she had to move out of Alan Humphrey's house. It would be perfect.

On Thursday morning, Alice unlocked the

door of the youth centre, pleased to see that the boxes she expected to be delivered yesterday had arrived. She busied herself setting up the new computers and keyboards along the bench that had been built along the back wall of the new centre. The electrician had been there a couple of days ago and had put in four double power points behind it. By the time lunchtime rolled around, Tilly and Jeremy arrived for their afternoon at the school in Augathella.

The door opened as they walked in, and Tilly grinned. 'Wow, you haven't been mucking around. Alice, it looks great!'

Jeremy walked straight over to the kitchen. 'Looks good in here too. You've done a lot of work this week, Alice. You've been busy.'

'Have you found somewhere to live yet?' Tilly asked.

'Yes, I've found a place about ten ks out of town, an old farmhouse on a property. I'm looking after it until the manager arrives.'

'Sounds like you're really settling in here in Augathella,' Jeremy said. 'Funny how we've all come home.'

'Yes, Augathella is starting to feel like home again to me already.'

'So, what's the plan for today?' Tilly asked. 'What time are we supposed to talk at the school?'

'I was hoping you and Jeremy could do it because I'd like to finish off here. We're opening up for after-school sessions this afternoon, and I've been to the butcher to order some sausages and the baker to get some bread rolls. If you guys want to finish at the school, you can come back here, and we can get a barbeque going at about 5 o'clock. That would be great.'

'Sounds good to me. So, we're at the school for the whole afternoon?' Jeremy clarified.

'Yes, they've got you talking to a few different groups, and the school counsellor is there. She's asked that you sit in on the talk she's giving to Year Ten.'

'Busy day,' Jeremy said.

'Do you want a coffee before you go?' Alice asked, heading over to put the kettle on.

'No, it's okay. We'll grab one at Janice's on the way,' Tilly said. 'Looks like you're busy. We'll head off to the school now and come back as soon as the day is over. See you then.'

Alice waved them off and went back to the last computer, loading in some login details for the kids.

The door opened, and she turned, wondering if they had forgotten something. But before anyone came in, the door closed again. She frowned and walked across to the door, opening it quietly. She stuck her head out just in time to see someone race around the back of the building.

Checking that she had her keys in her pocket, she locked the door behind her and headed quietly along the path that led to a grassed area around the back. Beau Burke was there, sitting on a stump next to the barbeque area. His hoodie was pulled over his face, and his shoulders were hunched.

'Hey, Beau, is that you?' she asked.

He turned to her, and his eyes were red. She could see the marks on his cheeks where tears had tracked down.

'Everything okay?'

He shook his head but didn't speak. Alice walked over and sat on the stump beside him. He lifted his arm and wiped the sleeve of his hoodie across his face.

'Can I stay here this afternoon?' he asked.

'Instead of going to school?' she asked.

'Yeah.'

'Is there a problem?'

'I just don't want to go.'

'What would your Uncle Billy say?' she asked.

'He said it was okay. He used to let me stay home when we were at Kununurra when the kids got to me.'

'Something happened at school?'

He lifted his head and looked at her, and it hit her in the chest how unhappy he looked.

'Will you tell me what's happened? I'm pretty sure I can organise for you to stay here today. I might just have to ring Billy and check it's alright.'

'You can't get him; his phone doesn't work right at the back of Jon's property. I tried to ring him to ask if I could go home.'

'I'm pleased to hear that you did that; it's good to get permission to do things.'

'Can I please stay here with you, Alice? Please?'

'Will you tell me what happened, mate?'

'There's a boy in our class, and he's been tormenting me about not having a mum. He's really cruel. Rory was gonna hit him, but I wouldn't let him.'

'But hitting isn't the answer, is it?'

'Probably not. Anyway, that's what I do. I don't like it. I just go—'

'Like the day you came down to Charleville when I met you.'

'Yeah, it was a good day to meet you. I'm happy we're friends now.'

'Okay, thank you for telling me what's wrong. There's only one thing—if you stay here with me today, I'll have to call the school and tell them where you are.'

'That's okay,' he mumbled.

After the fabulous night she had at the Cartwrights last weekend and a good week with a lot achieved at the new branch of the youth centre, Alice's equilibrium was restored.

Friday night rolled around, and she asked Jeremy and Tilly what their plans were for the night.

'I'm going to have dinner at the bistro at the pub,' she said. 'If you'd like to join me.'

'Would love to, Alice,' Tilly said, 'but we've already made plans for tonight down in Charleville.'

'No problem at all,' Alice said. 'We'll do it another night.'

'For sure, take a rain check.'

Alice was still staying at the pub until she moved out to Alan Humphreys' property. She was taking the rest of her things out there on Sunday afternoon. She hadn't been able to settle all week, and she couldn't put her finger on what was causing her restlessness. Usually, after a day down at Charleville, when she got back to the flat, she would be happy to collapse in front of the television or with a book and a glass of wine after cooking her dinner, followed by an early night. But the past couple of weeks, she'd found it hard to settle. Last night, she'd looked around the hotel room and couldn't wait to get out to Alan's place. Maybe she'd have more to do out there for a night and a weekend, but it was Friday night, and she certainly wasn't going to stay alone in the hotel room.

Surely, there'd be somebody down in the bistro that she knew. She'd been disappointed when Jeremy and Tilly couldn't join her because they were such great company. She didn't feel comfortable asking Bec. Even though they worked closely, Bec was still the boss, and Alice was still a little bit shy. She knew her place in the employment scheme of things.

Today had been quiet at the centre. Everyone was pretty sure that the fundraising from the ball would be going towards the centre, and everyone Alice talked to had agreed it was the best cause. Mind you, she hadn't talked to Gladys, who was still telling all and sundry that they all needed televisions in their rooms at the aged care facility. Tilly had pulled Alice aside and told her to ignore it. She said if Nana wanted her own television, she could well afford to buy one. She said it was just that she wanted to have a say, but she knew her grandmother loved going out to the communal area to watch television with all the other people in the home.

'Just ignore her, Alice. Don't let her get under your skin.'

'Was I that obvious the other day?' Alice asked, pulling a face.

'You didn't say anything, you were very well-behaved. She's always been used to calling the shots. I was really surprised when Beryl stood up to her last week, too. But listen, I'm sorry we can't come tonight. You go out and have a good time.'

Alice had thought about it when she got home and decided she would. She ran a deep bath, grabbed a glass of wine, and sat back in the refurbished bathroom at the hotel. After getting out, drying off, and getting dressed, she realised that she hadn't booked a table. Well, surely she wouldn't need to book a table for one, but being Friday night, though, you never know. It was a bistro with a dining room, and it could be busy, as there seemed to be a lot of functions on these days. Well, if she had to, she could go and get a hamburger—so be it.

She stood at the wardrobe debating what to wear. She reached into the wardrobe and pulled out her dress. Now that the weather was warming up, that would be good with a cardigan tonight. It was a pretty dress with a sweetheart neckline and a swirly bottom, with a pattern of primary colours that sort of looked like flowers but were really just blobs.

She didn't bother much more. She pulled the clip out of her hair that she'd tied up in the bath and ran a brush through it. A smudge of lipstick and a dash of mascara, she slipped on her pink sandals and headed down the carpeted steps.

She frowned as she reached the bottom step that led into the hall that entered the bistro. It was very quiet. They should be open; they opened every night except Monday. She walked along quickly and pushed open the door. To her surprise, the bistro and the dining room were both empty.

She went over to the counter, where a waitress was polishing the cutlery. 'Is there a function on tonight?' she asked hesitantly.

'No, there's a party over at New Life. One of the old folks from the aged care facility is having his eightieth, and Chloe and Rosie offered to cater because they thought it would be more private for them than here at the pub on a Friday night.'

The waitress rolled her eyes. 'The night's gonna take forever to go. There's nobody booked in for dinner. Not one. Most of the town's going to the party. How come you're not?' she asked Alice with a face screwed up.

'Because I don't know many people in town. I'm staying upstairs in the pub until I move out on Sunday.'

The young girl tilted her head to the side. 'Oh, I know you—you're working at that youth centre thing.'

'Yep, that's me.'

'And you're gonna be living at Alan's. Are you Alice?'

'I am. I thought I might meet some of my friends here, but it looks like they might have gone to the birthday party as well.'

'Probably. Even my folks have gone,' the young girl said. 'It's gonna be massive. But don't worry, you won't be in the dining room by yourself. There's one bloke in there already. He put his order in, but Sean had to run down to the

New Life Centre because he was helping Chloe with some dish or other.'

'Are there any specials on tonight?' Alice asked.

The young girl shook her head. 'No, just the normal menu.'

'I'll take one with me and look when I sit down. What's your name?' Alice asked.

'I'm Jules, and I'll be looking after you tonight. I'll be your waitress,' she said in a spiel that she obviously polished when the place was crowded.

'Thanks, Jules. I will.'

'Would you like a drink? I'll go to the bar and do one for you.'

'A glass of white wine would be very nice.'

The girl tilted her head to the other side this time. 'Riesling, Semillon, or Chardonnay?'

'Riesling would be fine, thank you.' Alice hid a grin at the eighteen-year-old waitress who knew all the white wines.

'Okay, sit down and here's your menu. I'll be back in a minute to take your order.'

Alice walked slowly to the bistro. Tonight wasn't panning out as she planned. She was sure that someone from the school or one of the properties would've been here tonight, but it looked like she was going to have an early meal and head back up to her room. She let out a sigh. More streaming television. She was never going to meet anyone this way.

She looked over at her favourite table by the window, where at least she could look out on the beer garden and the paddocks. The sun hadn't set yet, and the days were getting longer as spring approached.

She crossed the room, and an amused voice called out to her. 'Miss Templeton?'

Goosebumps ran up her arms. She knew that voice—it couldn't be. . . .

She turned slightly towards the side wall, and sure enough, Billy Burke was sitting at the table near the door with an open newspaper in front of him.

A wide grin split his face, and the laughter lines she noticed around his eyes the other evening crinkled.

'Hello, Mr Burke,' she said.

'I thought we agreed to make it Billy and Alice,' he said.

'Well, you called me Miss Templeton,' she retorted.

He put both his hands up in peace. 'I forgot, sorry. But remember, we're friends now.'

A smile crept over Alice's face. 'We are.' She was suddenly pleased she'd put on her prettiest dress and lipstick and brushed her hair.

'Are you meeting someone?' he asked. 'I'm sorry, that's probably none of my business.'

'No,' she said. 'I decided I didn't want to spend the night holed up in my room, getting takeaway and watching television five nights in a row, so I decided to come down and have dinner.' She pulled a face. 'Although I was hoping I'd know somebody here tonight. I mean...' She realised what she said. 'I mean, I thought there might be some groups of friends here having dinner. Apparently, there's some big party on in town.' She looked around the room. 'Where's Beau? Is he okay?'

'Yes, he's fine and as happy as because he's having a sleepover at the Cartwrights.' Billy's eyes met hers, and she found it hard to look away. Without that five o'clock shadow, he looked younger. Her gaze moved down to the snug navy blue T-shirt he wore. Then she realised what she was doing and quickly looked up. A glimmer of a smile tipped his lips as he spoke.

'That's good.' The silence was awkward for a minute as Alice stood there. She looked around again. 'It is very quiet in here tonight.'

'I was thinking the same thing, but it looks like it's going to be a quiet night everywhere in town tonight due to that party. Young Jules there tells me that there are no other bookings. I was pleased to see another customer arrive. And even more so when I realised it was you.' Billy pushed his newspaper aside, and his chair scraped on the wooden floorboards as he stood up. 'May I have the pleasure of your company for dinner, Alice?' he asked.

A strange feeling shimmied down her arms and legs, and she couldn't help but answer quickly. If she had taken time to think about it, she would have said no, and that would have appeared rude. Why should she give up the idea of company and having dinner with an attractive man just because of one difficult encounter? As he said, they had made up and, if not exactly friends, at least they were no longer adversaries. They both had Beau's well-being at heart.

'I would be delighted to have dinner with you, Mr…' she hesitated and smiled. 'Billy.'

He came around and pulled out a chair for her. 'Take a seat, please, Alice. May I get you a drink?'

CHAPTER 27

Jules came back over but without Alice's glass of wine. 'I came back to check whether you really want wine,' she said, tapping her pencil against the order pad. 'I've picked you as a G&T girl.'

'Do you know what?' Alice said. 'That sounds tempting. I'll change my order. I'm upstairs tonight, so I don't have to worry about driving home. So, yes, please, a gin and tonic.'

'Jules, have you got the orders yet?'

Alice looked past the waitress to the ordering alcove beside the new commercial kitchen. She had to force her mouth to stay closed as her eyes settled on the new chef. Jules simply ignored him.

'Yeah, not bad, is he?' Jules commented with a glance in the chef's direction. 'He could be on one of those TV shows, I reckon.'

'Who is he?' Alice asked. 'I haven't seen him round town before.'

'He's the new chef. Bit of a honey, hey?'

Alice nodded and thought to herself, he certainly is a bit of a honey. A chef—hmmm, that's a profession. Hospitality hours weren't the best, but it's still a profession.'

Jules gave a slow grin. 'I can see exactly what you're thinking, but don't get your hopes up, love. He's married.'

Alice tried to compose her features into a serious look. 'What did you think I was thinking?' She blushed as she caught Billy's eyes on her.

'I could read your face, love,' Jules said.

Billy grinned. 'Me too.'

'Okay, I admit it. I was thinking what a nice-looking young man he was and wondering if he was new to town. That was all.'

'Sadly, he's married. His wife's a ringer out at Jon Ingram's place.'

'Interesting combination. Chef and ringer.'

'Like me and my partner,' Jules said. 'I'm an Augathella girl. You're both new to town, aren't you? I didn't realise you were together.'

'We're not.' Alice and Billy said at the same time.'

'Oh, okay. But you are going to sit here?'

Alice hoped Billy didn't see the big wink that Jules sent her way. She nodded. 'Yes, we know each other.'

Billy was looking from one to the other, still

smiling.

Jules settled in for a chat and ignored the dagger looks that the chef was sending her way. Alice half expected her to pull out a chair for a minute.

'I grew up here,' Alice said. 'On a property, but now I'm working here and in Charleville, too. I decided to take a room in the pub until I move to a property on Allenvale Road in a week or so. What about you?'

'I grew up here too.' Jules flicked a glance back to the kitchen but kept talking. 'I'm younger than you. My partner came to town. I met him here in the pub one night a few months back. He's a tax agent. He goes around all the small towns. Tax time keeps him busy.'

'Where's he based?' Alice asked.

'Longreach,' she said. 'I guess I'll move there when we get married.'

'You're engaged?' Alice looked at Jules' hand, but there was no ring on it.

'No, but we're going to be. I've made up my mind,' she said, 'to get out of this hick town.'

'It's come a long way since I lived here,' Alice said.

'Yeah, I gotta admit, there's a lot more to do

here now, but you know, when you grow up somewhere, you want to go and try something else.'

'Yes, I did that.' Alice was aware of Billy's interest as she spoke.

'Anyway, I better take your order before Robbo loses his cool. He's got a bit of a temper,' Jules said.

Billy chuckled. 'We haven't looked at the menu yet.'

***

'Can I buy your drink?' Billy was still grinning as Jules walked away.

Alice chuckled. 'Thank you, but I'm fine. May I get you a drink when she brings mine out?' She noticed that his beer glass was almost empty.

'Are you going to drink wine with dinner?' he asked.

'Possibly,' she said. 'I don't have to drive tonight. What about you, with Beau?'

'Friday night out at the pub has become quite a habit,' he said. 'A regular date. Braden invites me to stay over, too, but I know he and Callie have got their hands full, and he works so hard. I'm sure they would appreciate having a night to themselves without a third wheel. Besides, I

214

think Beau is a little bit more relaxed when I'm not around.'

'How are you both getting on?' she asked. 'And I'm asking as a friend, nothing official, okay? Don't take it the wrong way.'

'I know. You don't look like Alice Templeton at work tonight.'

'Should I take that as a compliment or not?' Her face reddened as she felt the heat rise into her cheeks. 'I'm not fishing for compliments. Please don't take it the wrong way.'

'You look very pretty tonight, Alice. I find it hard to connect you with the woman with the tight bun and the navy blue suit.'

'I got dressed up that day because I had a meeting down at the council in Charleville. You'll rarely see me in a business suit.' She chuckled. 'You were just lucky, Billy, that you met me that day. Maybe you wouldn't have taken me so seriously if I had a dress like this on.'

'Maybe not,' he said.

'You never know. Anyway, I wasn't digging. Tell me, how's it going with you two?'

Before he could answer, Jules arrived at the table and placed a large glass in front of Alice.

'Oh, wow, that's a big one,' she said.

Jules winked again and nudged Alice with her elbow after she put the drink on the table. 'I made it a double to save you some money,' she said.

'You didn't have to do that.'

'Well, you don't have to drive home, do you?'

'Thank you, Jules. Put the drinks on my tab,' Billy said.

'So, are you ready to order yet?' Jules grinned and looked back at the kitchen, where the chef could be seen hovering at the small alcove.

'No, give us five minutes, thanks,' Billy said. 'We still haven't had a chance to have a look.' He winked at Alice as Jules walked away.

'Do you work with the chef's wife?'

'I do. Noreen is one of the new ringers.'

'It's an unusual combination.'

'These days, anything goes,' Billy said. 'I've seen lots of different setups as I worked around the properties in the NT and here. Head stockman at the big spread over there was married to the lawyer in town.'

'I guess I'm too judgmental,' she said.

'How long were you on your farm?'

'Mum and Dad passed away and left the farm to me. I sold it because I didn't want to spend my life there. And I couldn't afford the mortgage repayments.'

'Regretting it now a little bit? Do I pick up a hint of nostalgia in your tone?'

'Really, I think that's because I'd like to put some roots down. And I think Augathella will be the place where I do it.'

'When are you moving into Alan's place?' he asked.

'Not sure yet,' she said. 'I've decided to stay here at the pub for a few nights instead of going backwards and forwards to Charleville. Alan kindly let me put some of my things in the shed so I can stay at the pub until I move in.'

'So you can let your hair down tonight. Shame there's no music on. You didn't know about the birthday party either?'

'No,' she said. 'There are a lot of new people in town that I don't know. When I came back from travelling overseas, I lived in Brisbane before I moved to Charleville. I lost touch with a lot of my friends. Since I got involved with the organisation of the spring ball, I've met a lot of the girls again. Some of them I went to school with, but most of them are younger than me.'

'How old are you? I thought you'd not long left school.'

'Ha ha.' She gave him a coquettish look and then put her head to the side and a finger to her cheek. 'Is that a question you ask a lady?'

'Perhaps not. I was curious. You seem to have done a lot. I'm thirty-four, so you don't have to ask me my age,' Billy said.

'Okay, then. I'm almost thirty-three,' she said.

'Well, you certainly don't look it. Tonight, you look about twenty-one.'

'Flattery will get you everywhere, Mr Burke.' It had been a long time since she'd flirted, and Alice was enjoying herself. She took a big sip of her drink. Wow, Jules had been heavy-handed.

As if her thoughts summoned her to the table, Jules came back to the table. 'Have you had a look at the menu yet? Robbo's getting a bit antsy,' she said. 'If he feeds you now, he can have an early night.'

Alice shook her head. 'No, he can't. I'm out for dinner to have a nice meal. I'll probably have an entrée, a main and a dessert, so let the chef know we'll probably be here for quite a while.'

'Well, hurry up and choose so we can at least get started in the kitchen.' As Jules spoke, a group of six older people came through the door.

'Looks like you're going to have a busier night than you were expecting,' Billy said.

'Bloody grey nomads,' Jules said. 'They always come late. Anyway, I don't mind. I'd rather be busy. Now, it might be wise to have a look at the menu and pick what you want. Otherwise, if these guys get their orders in before you, you might be waiting a while.'

'Are you in a hurry, Alice?' Billy's smile was cheeky.

She grinned back. 'No, are you?'

Alice picked up the menu that was in front of her. Nerves trembled in her arms and legs as Billy held her gaze across the table.

'Would you like to buy a couple of entrées and share them?' Billy asked.

'Sounds good to me. What do you like to eat?' she asked.

'Well, being a long way from the sea, I'm always reluctant to buy anything seafood because it's inevitably battered and deep-fried. Did you see the venison on the menu?'

Alice quickly scanned the laminated menu. 'It sounds good, doesn't it? Okay, I'll order that. And what are you going to order?'

'I think I'll have the deep-fried camembert.' The next five minutes were spent discussing the various options on the menu, and they were totally relaxed with each other by the time Jules came over to finally take their order and deliver another gin and tonic for Alice, as well as a beer for Billy.

'Would you like wine with your dinner?' Billy looked at the schooner of beer that was sitting in front of him on the table.

'What about you?' she asked. 'I certainly can't drink a bottle by myself.'

'Well, I guess if I drink this schooner, I'm not going to be able to drive home for quite a few hours, so why not? What wine would you like, Alice? Red or white?'

'Well, we're sharing the venison and I'm having the steak. I think I'd like to go with red. How about you, Billy?'

'Sounds good to me.'

Alice watched as Jules handed him the wine list, and he looked at it. 'Yes, I've had that one before. Let's go for the Hunter Valley Merlot.

Not too heavy. Is that okay with you, Alice?'

'Sounds good.' As Jules took their order and walked away, Alice looked at him curiously. 'You know your wines.'

'One of my hobbies,' he said. 'I'm not just a beer-swilling stockman.' But his tone was light, and she knew he hadn't taken offence.

By the time Jules brought out one sticky date pudding and a pannacotta for Alice, she and Billy were firm friends. She had gone slowly on the wine, but the two strong gins and the two glasses of wine had certainly had an effect and relaxed her even more. She found herself looking at Billy, her gaze lingering each time and enjoying that pleasant feeling running through her bloodstream.

'Just the wine talking,' she chided herself silently.

By the time they finished dessert, there were a couple of glasses of wine left in the bottle, and Jules and Robbo, the chef, were packing up.

'Would you like to go out and sit in the garden and finish the wine?' Billy asked.

'That would be lovely,' Alice said.

Billy picked up the wine and the two glasses in one hand and waited for her to stand. He followed her out of the side door of the bistro into the beer garden with his hand on her elbow. Her skin burned where his fingers gently touched her.

Calm down, girl. It has been a long time since you've been with anyone

Was that the only reason she was having such a physical reaction to his touch?

Then again, if she was honest, she had the same physical reaction every time he looked at her and as he'd told her more about himself over dinner. He was a good-looking man, and she had now decided he was a very nice man. 'Nice is a terrible word,' she remembered her school teacher saying in primary school. Okay, he was a great guy, and she was really enjoying his company.

As they reached the table in the far corner with the best view of the moon over the pub's roof, he put the glasses and the bottle down, but she didn't move, and his body brushed against her. Billy hesitated as he stood back, and somehow, his other hand moved to her, and he pulled her close.

'Thank you for your company, Alice. I really enjoyed myself,' he said quietly as she stared up at him, his features outlined by the soft moonlight.

Alice couldn't help herself. She stood on her toes and brushed her lips against his. 'Thank you, Billy. I've enjoyed myself too.'

'I guess before we sit down and finish that bottle of wine, I better go and make sure I can get myself a room here; otherwise, I'll be camping in the back of the ute.'

Alice didn't hesitate. She'd let too many opportunities pass in her lifetime, opportunities that she regretted. If she had taken them up, who knew—she could be a married woman by now with a couple of kids.

'I have a king-size bed in my room,' she said slowly. 'I'm sure there's plenty of room for two.'

Billy's eyes widened, and a sexy smile lifted his lips.

'Are you sure about that?' he asked, pulling her closer before his lips met hers.

CHAPTER 28

On Monday morning, Alice was still smiling when she closed the door of her hotel room behind her and headed down to the youth centre.

Friday night had been unbelievable, and there had been no embarrassment when she had woken with Billy beside her the next morning. He'd stayed until mid-morning, and the kiss they'd shared at the door told her how much he'd enjoyed their dinner and the rest of the night.

'I really enjoyed myself too,' she said, her voice a little shy.

'Can I ask you out for a real date next time Beau goes out to stay at the Cartwrights?'

Alice hesitated for only a second, and a smile tilted her lips.

'That would be lovely,' she said, 'but remember I won't be here past Wednesday. I'll be staying at Alan Humphreys' house for a few weeks.'

'Even better,' he said. 'That's not terribly far from where I am at the Ingram's. I can pick you up, and we could come into town.'

What remained unspoken was that they

would spend another night together, but Alice crossed her fingers behind her back as Billy kissed her goodbye again.

'I better go,' he said reluctantly. 'I have to pick Beau up.'

Tilly was already in the centre when Alice arrived, and the aroma of fragrant coffee greeted Alice. She pushed the door open, smoothed her hands down her shirt and jeans—she had dressed casually this morning—and stepped inside.

'Well, hello,' Tilly said. 'Don't you look lovely? Looks like you had a very relaxing weekend. You haven't moved out to your new place yet?' she asked.

'No, I went out and had a look, but Alan wants me to wait until new carpet is laid in the bedroom and living room. I said to him it didn't matter, but I'm happy to wait. I'm staying at the pub in town.'

'I thought you might've been at the party on Friday night.'

'No, I didn't know whose party it was,' she said, 'but I had dinner at the pub. It was lovely.' She couldn't help the blush that heated her cheeks.

'Did you see the new chef, Robbo? What a

looker.' Tilly pretended to fan herself. 'If I weren't taken, I'd be spending my time there too.'

'He's married,' Alice said.

'Really? What a waste. Okay, take him off your list.'

'He wasn't on it,' Alice said with a secret smile as she crossed the room to the coffee machine. 'What's on the agenda today?' she asked.

The week flew by. The youth centre was busy, and a lot more of the local youth were getting involved as each day passed. The ball was coming up quickly; it was now only three weeks away. Alice had sewing to do each night. They had now made over three hundred masks. Surely that was enough, she thought as she added the last one to the pile at the end of a week of hard work and constant sewing. The committee held weekly meetings now, and progress was made each week. Callie was a great chairperson and managed to keep Gladys Tingle in line, much to Tilly's relief.

'Honestly, she's getting worse as she gets older. Maybe she's learning bad habits in that aged care facility,' Tilly said at morning tea at the youth centre on Wednesday morning. The meeting at Jenna's Tearoom yesterday afternoon had been relatively heated, but Callie had kept the peace.

'Your grandma's all right,' Alice said. 'She's just lonely. She likes to have her say.'

'She certainly does.' But Alice's kindness towards Gladys Tingle disappeared very quickly at the end of that meeting.

Gladys picked her time very well. She waited till everybody was there and having coffee before Callie started the meeting.

'I hear you had dinner at the pub with Billy Burke on Friday night, Alice,' Gladys said, her lips pursed in disapproval.

Alice was wearing a red T-shirt, and she was sure that her face was the same colour as her T-shirt when everybody turned to look at her. Gladys was the only one looking at her disapprovingly; several other faces had delighted smiles.

It's none of your business, Gladys, Alice thought as she kept a bright smile on her face.

Tilly caught her eye and nodded. 'Aha,' she said.

Gladys picked up on it quickly. 'Aha what,

Tilly?'

'Nothing, I was just clearing my throat.'

'And that's not all I heard,' Gladys said. 'The next morning—'

Alice put down her coffee cup with a loud thud on the table. She turned to Callie. 'Perhaps we could get the meeting started now, Callie. We have a lot to get through, Gladys,' she said, her voice tight.

Tilly leaned and whispered in her grandmother's ear, and she obviously said something that made Gladys shut up, much to Alice's great relief.

If Gladys Tingle knew that Billy Burke had been seen leaving her room on Saturday morning—and she was sure he had been very cautious in getting out to his car—then she had probably told the whole town by now.

Anyway, no one could confirm he had been in her room; there were plenty of vacant rooms that night, so who was to say they shared a room? Not that it was any of their business. She'd had a fantastic night, and if anyone wanted to talk about it, she'd be pretty upfront and tell them it *was* none of their business.

After Gladys's interruption, Tuesday

afternoon's meeting flew by, and by the time the meeting closed at five p.m. things were sorted.

'The masks have all gone. We need to get another fifty or so made in the next week. Thanks to everyone who volunteered,' Callie said. 'And the ticket sales are going brilliantly. We're up over three hundred now.'

As it was a weekday afternoon, everyone packed up and left quickly, and Alice and Callie were the only ones left. Alice helped Callie carry the empty coffee cups over to the kitchen for Gemma, and Callie smiled.

'I'm pleased to hear that you and Billy had dinner together the other night. It'll be good for him to get to know somebody.' Callie smiled. 'Oh, and just so you know, in case you want to do it again, Beau's staying at our place on Friday night.' Alice put her head down and carried the next cups to the kitchen.

***

'Billy, watch out!' Braden called. Billy pulled up his horse just in time before it stumbled at the end of the creek bed.

He shook himself. 'Sorry, mate, my mind was elsewhere.'

'Beau giving you grief again?' Braden said.

'No,' Billy shook his head. 'He's been great. He's even started calling me Uncle Billy all the time now, not only when he wants something.'

'Everything okay?'

Billy's grin was broad. 'Everything is pretty good.' He had found himself daydreaming over the past few days, and a couple of times, he picked up his phone to call Alice. They had exchanged numbers on Saturday morning because he was going to ring her up and pick a night for them to go out.

When he picked up Beau on Saturday afternoon, Billy was as pumped as Beau was after a whole day of football.

Callie had put her hand on Billy's arm before they headed to the car and said, 'How about another sleepover next Friday night? It's good for my boys to have company other than each other,' she said.

Normally, Billy would have hesitated, but the thought of another night out with Alice won out.

'That would be great, Callie. Thank you so much.'

'And the same as last week,' she said. 'You're quite welcome to stay the night. If you don't feel comfortable staying in the house, bring your swag.'

Billy grinned as he compared sleeping in his swag at the back of Braden and Callie's shed to sharing a room with Alice Templeton.

'It's good for Billy and me to have some time apart. If that suits you, we'll make Friday night a date.'

'I'll let the boys know tomorrow.'

'Thanks, Callie. I really appreciate it,' Billy said. 'I'll tell Beau.'

He held off ringing Alice until Wednesday morning. She answered quickly, and he wondered if it was because she'd recognised his number.

'Hey, Billy, how are you?' she said.

'I'm great, thank you. How are you?'

'I'm great too,' she said.

'That's good.'

He wondered whether he was rushing too much.

'Did you have a night in mind for us to have the next date?' she asked

His voice held steady. 'Yes, Beau's staying out at the Cartwright's again on Friday night. I was wondering if I could pick you up and bring you into town for a meal.'

She was quiet for a moment. 'Well, look, instead of driving into town and making a bit of a spectacle of ourselves again, how about I cook dinner at my new place? Apparently, Gladys Tingle saw us, or someone told her that we were there. I'll have to have a word with Jules. Plus, it's not so far for you to drive home.'

He nodded, 'Okay, we'll see what the night brings. I'd love to have dinner there, but one more question.'

'Yes?' she asked, her voice sounding worried.

'Can you cook, or do I need to bring a barbeque?'

'I'll have you know that I'm a very good cook,' she said

'They say the way to a man's heart is through his stomach.'

Why did he say that? He was turning into some sort of romancing pansy.

Alice Templeton had been in his thoughts since he walked out of her hotel room on Saturday morning, and no matter how he tried, he couldn't get her out of his head.

CHAPTER 29

Beau's sleepover at the Cartwrights' became a regular Friday night event, as did Billy's sleepover at Alice's place every Friday night. Alice was walking on air most of the time, experiencing feelings she'd never felt before. She'd had boyfriends before, and she'd gotten over them when they'd moved on, even Rafe, who had held her heart until she'd realised it was a one-sided affair, but the time she was spending with Billy was fantastic. And it wasn't only the physical side of their relationship—it was the kind and gentle man that he was that made her smile and long to spend more time with him.

Billy had opened up about his past, and she learned how he left Mount Isa as a young boy and went to work on the land before he went to university. He'd tried a few other things, he told her, but he hadnF't gone into detail because many of their conversations never finished. They ended up in the bedroom, and there wasn't a lot of talking.

The fourth Friday night they spent together was in mid-September, only a week before the Masquerade Ball.

Billy wanted to know what she was going to do when she had to move from the farm. It wouldn't be long before she had to move out because Alan Humphreys had called to say the new manager was arriving soon. She had to decide whether she was going to buy a place or rent again.

But Alice knew she had bigger decisions to make.

As much as she loved spending time with Billy, he wasn't the man she could spend the rest of her life with. She wouldn't marry anyone connected with the land; she'd seen what it had done to Dad. She loved the time she spent with Billy, but there had been no talk of a future, so she didn't have to worry about it.

She shook herself out of her thoughts as she parked at the New Life store, where the ball was being held.

The meeting room at the side of the store was crammed with people. The committee had grown over the past weeks as more volunteers had joined up to help on the night. Callie stood with her hands resting on her pregnant tummy, and Alice hoped that she wouldn't go to the hospital before the ball. Callie had been the glue that held this whole committee together as president, and with her agenda, she had addressed absolutely everything they could think of.

'You're not going to have that baby before the ball, are you?' Alice asked.

Callie chuckled.'No, I'm just huge. I've still got two months to go yet.'

'You're not having twins again, are you, Callie?' Gladys Tingle asked.

'Thank goodness, no. It's only one baby,' Callie said.

'Must be a boy,' Gladys said.

'Must be,' Callie said with a patient smile.

Alice kept glancing at the time on her phone as the meeting seemed to go on forever. Time dragged on as they discussed all the final details, such as how much milk to buy and what time Chloe and Rosie would be opening up the department store for them to clear the bottom floor to extend the function centre.

Many women had volunteered their husbands and sons to help move the stock and put the chairs in, so there was a sitting room outside of the dance area on the night of the ball.

Finally, just before six, Callie called the meeting to a halt. 'Well, ladies, can I just say what a tremendous job you've all done?'

Gladys Tingle stood up and shook her head. Callie turned to face her, and Alice stared, her mouth open, wondering what Gladys was up to now.

'All of *us*,' the elderly lady said. 'Now, I'd like to say a few words, Callie. I'd like to formally move that we thank Callie for the wonderful job she's done as president and how she's kept us all on the straight and narrow.' Gladys chuckled. 'Beryl told me how difficult I can be sometimes, and Tilly keeps me in line, too. But Callie, you've done a fine job, and the success of this ball rests on your shoulders.'

Callie smiled and shook her head. 'Thank you, Gladys. It was a group effort, but I've really enjoyed being president. But,' she patted her tummy, 'it will be nice to step down and have a bit of a rest. School holidays start the day after the ball, and I intend on putting my feet up for two weeks.'

When the meeting was over, Alice waited beside her car for Bec to come out to the car park. The car park was almost empty as everyone had left to go home before dark. Spring was almost here, and the air was fragrant with the smell of the roses growing on a trellis at the back of the car park. Not only had Chloe's group provided a store for the community, but they had beautified much of the town with new gardens.

She waved as Bec walked across towards her car. 'Bec, can I have a quick word?'

'Hi, Alice. Hard to believe that was our second last meeting.'

'I'm sure we'll have a follow-up after the ball. I've got used to our afternoon meetings in town.'

'And how lovely was our Gladys this afternoon?' Bec grinned. 'You haven't had any more run-ins with her?'

'Don't talk about it. I'm sure she has spies all over town.' Alice chuckled.

'I was really pleased to hear you've been going out a bit. You've been working too hard.'

'Speaking of that,' Alice said, 'I was hoping I could take a couple of hours off tomorrow afternoon. I need to put together some new furniture that's being delivered. I didn't know it was going to be one of those "follow the instructions to put together" cupboards.' she said. 'Jeremy and Tilly are both happy to stay till five o'clock for the after-school crowd at the centre.'

'Yeah, look, take all afternoon if you want,' she said. 'That's not a problem at all. You've got so many hours up your sleeves, even since the camp.'

'No, I'm not worried about that,' Alice said, 'but a couple of hours would be great.'

'Do you need a hand out there? Can I send Matt over to help you?'

'It's all good. Billy and Beau are coming over to help me with it.'

Bec looked at her with a smile. 'Are you going to the ball with Billy Burke?'

Alice stared at Bec. 'I . . . I don't know. Why?'

'I thought you were a couple these days. Small town, remember, and we do have Gladys, who keeps everyone up to date with what's happening in town.'

Alice folded her arms. 'I don't even live in town anymore!'

Bec chuckled. 'Gladys doesn't miss a trick. So is she right?'

'We've spent a bit of time together.' Alice's face heated. 'I hope that's okay, having time with someone socially,' she said. 'I did start off with

Billy in an official capacity.'

'You bring too much of your old job to this one, Alice,' Bec said. 'Remember, they're not clients; they're just kids who come to the centre. How's young Beau going, anyway?'

Alice was pleased to get off the subject of her relationship with Billy.'By all accounts, he's going really well. Billy told me the other night that he was getting some extra tutoring because he was getting picked on a bit at school. I had him at the centre one day, and I had to ring the school and tell them that was okay. They actually sent over one of the teacher's aides to work with him offsite.'

'They run a good outfit there at the primary school. They wouldn't let anyone fall behind. Anyway, happy furniture making, and I'll see you at our final meeting on Friday afternoon.'

'Thanks, Bec. I really appreciate it.'

CHAPTER 30

Beau chatted non-stop to Billy from the minute he picked him up at the bus stop at the Ingram's front gate, and he climbed into the ute.

'There's a sandwich and a can of lemonade in the cooler between the seats,' Billy said as Beau clicked his seatbelt on. 'Grab some of that if you're hungry.'

'Why are we going back into town? I could've stayed in there.'

'No, we're going to Alice's place to help her put some furniture together.'

'Oh, cool! I wonder if she's got a computer at her house or maybe a game console.'

'Did you hear what I said, Beau? We're going to help her, not socialise or play games. She needs two men to help her put a cupboard together. You might learn some new skills that don't involve looking at a screen.'

Beau's chest puffed out. 'I can help do that. I'm a quick learner. Coops told me today I'm nearly caught up.'

'That's great. Plus, you're growing like a weed. Some of that food you're eating is finally starting to settle on your bones. You look really good, mate.'

'You know what it is, Uncle Billy?' Beau leaned forward and put his hands on the dashboard as they turned onto the road that led the five kilometres to Alice's place. 'I think it's because I've got friends.'

'And you reckon that might put weight on your bones?'

'No, I think it's because I'm happy. I don't spend all my time worrying.'

Billy lifted his hand off Beau's hair. 'It's good to hear that, mate. Not good to be worrying.'

'I know. I miss Mum, and I'll never forget her. I really wish she was still here, but I guess moving down here has been really good. I've made friends. I've settled in at school really well, and I don't mind having you look after me now,' he said.

Billy's throat closed with emotion. 'Good to hear, mate. I have you for company, too.'

'Is Alice gonna be your girlfriend? Are you going to marry her one day? She'd make a great stepmum, just like Rory's mum. Did you know she wasn't his real mum?' was the next question, and the lump disappeared from Billy's throat as he almost choked, coughing.

'My girlfriend? Where on earth would you get that idea from?'

'Rory told me that he heard his mum and dad talking about you being her boyfriend and her being your girlfriend. Do you like her?'

'Of course, I like her. She's a nice person.'

'Why can't she be your girlfriend?'

'Well, I guess if we both wanted that, maybe she could, but it's early days yet, mate. I don't know her that well.'

'Mum used to say it didn't matter; you just knew the one.'

'The one? Who was she talking about?' Billy asked curiously.

'I always hoped it was my dad, but I guess I'll never find out with Mum gone.'

'Probably not, mate, but listen, if you ever do want me to chase it up, I can do it for you.'

'No. Mum made me promise that I'd forget about it because she said if *she* didn't know, how the heck was I ever going to? How can you not know who gives you your baby?' His eyes were wide.

Billy swallowed again and searched for the

right words. 'I guess there are all sorts of things to do with that, mate, but we might talk about this when you get a bit older. You'll understand it better.'

Beau's face was a picture. 'I know what causes it; I've lived on farms all my life.'

Billy choked again. 'Yeah, but this isn't the time to be having this conversation. Look, we're at Alice's house now, and she's just pulled up in the driveway.'

Warmth suffused his chest as Alice stepped out of the car, her jeans snug and tight on her long legs. Her hair was loose on her shoulders, and his fingers itched to run through the soft, silky strands.

He had it bad.

CHAPTER 31

Alice parked near the shed at the farm, and it was only a few minutes before Billy and Beau pulled up in his ute. She had been sitting in her car, thinking about what Callie had said, but she couldn't quite come to terms with it. She knew what she didn't want, and before this situation with Billy got out of hand, she was going to have to make it quite clear to him.

She knew her voice was stilted as they approached her, and Billy's smile was wide. It still sent that usual mushy, warm, trembling feeling through all her limbs, but she refused to meet his gaze.

'Beau, if I give you my key, let yourself in the back door. I made some cakes last night, so there are some little cakes for your afternoon tea, and there's some chocolate milk on the fridge door. So, go and help yourself.'

Beau took the key from her. 'Thanks, Alice. You're a whiz. Do you have a com—'

'Beau.' Billy's voice held a warning.

Beau disappeared around the back of the house like a shot, and Billy reached over to put his arm around her, but Alice took a step back before he could kiss her.

'Everything okay?' Billy asked, his brow in a frown.

'Yes, yes, yes. I just wanted to have a bit of a talk with you, Billy. I'm a bit worried that I was leading you on too much.'

'Leading me on? What do you mean?'

'I don't want you to think that I'm after anything permanent or anything here.'

Alice looked down, and if she could have seen the look on Billy's face, maybe she would have reconsidered. By the time she looked up, Billy's mouth was set.

'Alice, I don't expect anything of you. I've just enjoyed your company.'

Enjoyed? So it was over already? That was easy, she thought as pain sliced through her chest. He hadn't expected anything of her. Did that mean that with one simple line like that, it was over?

'Anyway,' he said, 'We can't stay long as I have to help Jon with something this afternoon, so we only just came here to help you get that cupboard together.'

Oh. She had cooked dinner for them, but she

wasn't going to say that the aroma drifting from the slow cooker in the kitchen had been intended for them, too.

She forced a smile to her face. 'It's in the garage.' She took off across the yard, and Billy followed her.

Maybe it was for the best.

Beau and Billy put the cupboard together and carried it into the living room for her, which only took fifteen minutes. She probably should have left it in the shed because she was moving soon, but she wasn't going to get into a personal conversation with Billy this afternoon.

'Is there anything else you need a hand with?' he asked briskly.

'No, that's all, thank you.'

'Dinner smells good,' Beau said, obviously not noticing the tense atmosphere. 'Are we staying?'

'No, we're not,' Billy said tersely. 'Jump in the ute. I've got to go and help Jon.'

'I thought you said we'd stay here for tea?'

'No, I never said that, mate.'

'You didn't?'

'You can stay for dinner if you like,' Alice said quietly.

Billy replied, 'No need for that. See you around.'

Alice's heart broke as Billy looked at her—really looked at her—and she wondered if she had made a mistake.

'Are you going to the ball on Saturday night?' she asked hesitantly.

Before Billy could answer, Beau chimed in, 'We sure are! We've got our tickets, and I think Billy was even gonna ask you to come with us. Weren't you, Uncle Billy?'

Billy held Alice's gaze. 'I was, but I guess you would've said no.'

'No,' she shook her head. 'I wouldn't say no. That would be really nice, thank you.' She put her hand on Billy's arm. 'I would like to go with you.'

'I'm not sure if we'll be in town that night, Alice. I'll talk to you later. Come on, Beau.'

Her heart ached as they climbed into the ute and disappeared quickly in a puff of red dust.

***

Billy put his hand to his forehead before he crossed to the sink and rolled up his shirtsleeves.

Alice's words had broken him. He took out his frustration on the pots and scrubbed the

247

bottom of the burnt fry pan until he could see his reflection in it.

Beau walked in and picked up the tea towel. 'Not the best dinner you've cooked, Uncle Billy. If we'd had tea at Alice's, you wouldn't have a burnt pan to scrub.'

'Least of my worries, mate.'

'Why did you tell her you had to help Jon? He wasn't even home. You tell me not to lie.'

'Sometimes it's necessary, Beau.'

Beau shrugged and threw the teatowel onto the bench. 'Must be good to be grown up and do what you want. I'm going to do my homework. You're gonna be hours scrubbing that pan. I can still taste that burnt steak.'

Billy dropped his head into his hands.

Why was he such a coward? What the heck had he been thinking, taking Alice to bed and then thinking he could keep it casual?

She'd made it quite clear that was all she wanted. Where was he going to find the courage to let her go? He couldn't afford to trust what his heart was telling him.

Go and see her. Tell her you love her.

No, it would be easier to move on. He and Beau could move and start afresh somewhere else.

***

Alice put the contents of the slow cooker into containers and put them in the freezer.

Her mouth was dry, and her stomach was churning; she couldn't eat a thing. She knew she'd hurt Billy, and Beau was going to be collateral damage.

Confusion. Panic. Dread.

All the feelings running through her fought for precedence as she closed the freezer door.

More fool her, to blurt out to Billy that there was no future for them. Hell, he hadn't even offered one, and she'd come roaring in making assumptions. All because she was scared.

Now, Alice forced herself to step back and think about what she really wanted. Was it here on the farm that brought her unhappy memories back? Nights when Dad had looked exhausted as he stared out the window waiting for rain, and Mum had tried to tell him everything would be okay. Alice let the memories roll in; she had blocked so many unhappy memories. Tears ran down her face as she grieved for her parents.

But it hadn't been all right, and they had lost everything except the land and the house, which had been pretty much worthless back then.

Alice thought of the nights Billy had spent in her bed and the fun they'd had spending Sunday afternoons with Beau. The feeling that filled her when he'd held her in his arms.

She didn't want to be here without Billy. And Billy belonged on the land. Where did she want to be? Maybe she should move back to the city?

Her thoughts churned as she went to the bathroom and ran a deep bath.

Alice soaked in the hot water, letting it soothe her feelings. She'd fallen for Billy Burke, but there was no future there—not the future she wanted. He was an itinerant stockman with no home and an adopted child.

More fool her to get involved in the first place. Now Alice forced herself to step back and think about what she really wanted.

Could she move away? Or could she live here?

She sighed and closed her eyes.

CHAPTER 32

Tilly and Sophie had volunteered to help Jenna pack up the coffee cups and plates. Alice waited when Sophie called Callie over.

'Cal, a quick word before you go.'

Alice stood looking out over the paddocks as Sophie's excited voice reached her. The sky was a brilliant soft blue with shards of gold streaming from the low clouds to the west. The flat plains of the western region stretched as far as she could see to the north, broken only by the narrow ribbon of highway. The highway that beckoned to her. Maybe she'd be happier if she left. No matter how much she'd thought over the past few days, all she could think of was leaving Billy—and Beau—behind.

Callie's smile was wide when she approached the door, and they walked down to the car park together.

'You look happy,' Alice commented.

'Sophie's had some news from Jacinta, Kent's sister. Do you remember her?'

'I do. Didn't she work at the primary school for a while?'

'She did. But she moved to Brisbane when she met Ryan again. Maybe the strip show came to town before you moved back to the district?'

'Strip show?' Alice's eyes were wide. 'I don't think I recall a strip show in town?'

'A long story, but a good one with a happy ending. I'll tell you about it one day over a coffee. Ryan was the strip show manager. Anyway, he and Jacinta married a few years back, and she and Ryan have a little girl now. They don't get back here much because Ryan's second in charge of an international medical research establishment in Brisbane. The company has promoted him, and they're moving to Germany for a while.'

'That's a long way from Augathella,' Alice said slowly. 'Maybe I need to expand my horizons.'

Callie looked at her thoughtfully. 'Are you okay?'

'I'm fine. What about you? Are you going back to school after the holidays, Callie?'

'No.' Callie shook her head. 'I have my hands full with the twins. It's getting a bit hard to manoeuvre them now with this one.' She touched her belly.

'You are amazing, Callie,' Alice said.

'I'm not amazing, Alice. I'm just a woman who fell in love, found a family, and then made it bigger. My life is wonderful; I'm just so happy.'

Callie must have noticed the look on Alice's face because she put a hand on her wrist. 'Are you really okay, Alice? I know that you and Billy have been seeing each other.'

'Yes, we have, Callie, but there's no future in it. He's not what I want as a partner.'

'He's not?' Callie asked. 'Are you sure? I've seen the way you look at each other. You've both seemed so happy.'

'He's a really great guy, but he's not the one for me,' Alice said, 'but like I told you at that sewing bee we had at your place that afternoon, I don't want to marry or be with anyone on the land. I saw what it did to my dad. I want a professional man, someone who comes home every night with a briefcase and someone who works until five and has the weekends off.'

'You don't think you're dreaming too much, Alice?' Callie said.

'No, no, I know what I want.'

Callie kept her hand on Alice's arm. 'And

you know what I thought I wanted, Alice? I had a great job at a TV station in Brisbane. I had a beautiful home on the river, and I had all the money a girl could need. And you know what? The last thing I ever thought I'd need would be a widower with three young boys way out west, where I would never have dreamed of living. But love has different plans for us. When you meet the person you're destined to spend the rest of your life with, considerations like profession, money, and where you live all become very minor. If you truly love somebody, you will go where they want to go, and they will go where you want to go. Together, you work it out. And if it's the thought of Billy having young Beau that's holding you back, let me tell you that getting readymade sons when I fell in love with Braden was the icing on the cake.'

Alice looked down, her heart heavy.

'Callie, I've told myself all those things over and over again, but I still know what I don't want. It's deep in me; I can't let it go.'

'Perhaps, Alice, if things develop the way that I can see they are, perhaps you need to think about what you *do* want, not what you don't want.'

CHAPTER 33

Friday night would have been their sixth weekend together, but Alice told Billy she was busy. As well as their regular Friday night date, there had been Sunday afternoons when she, Billy, and Beau went for a picnic. They'd also been to a couple of weekend barbeques at the Cartwrights when she'd seen Callie looking at them thoughtfully. But when Tilly asked one afternoon if she and Billy were an item, Alice shook her head and said, 'No, we're just friends.'

Alice couldn't stand being trapped inside. As the sun set, a warm breeze drifted from the north. She decided to go out and pull the weeds along the front path. Her mind was full of Billy and the disappointment on Beau's face when they left early the other night. The meal she had cooked, expecting them to stay, had lasted her the next two nights, and there was still enough in the freezer for tonight.

She paused, her heart heavy, and pushed herself to her feet. There was a loud noise coming from a long way away. She stood still, as a ball of dust rose in the east. Then she realised the sound was that of an ambulance roaring up the dirt road. Her heart lodged in her throat, and she wondered where it was going because it was undoubtedly in a hurry. By the time she walked to the gate, it had covered the road at tremendous speed, dust kicking up behind it as the siren blared and the lights flashed. It sped past her house in a whiz, disappearing to the west in the direction of Jon and Fallon's property.

She felt sick to her stomach. There were no other properties at the end of that road—Jon and Fallon's was the last one, and that's where Billy and Beau lived, in the house down the back. Someone had had an accident, and the chance that it was somebody she knew, somebody she cared about, someone she had rejected, filled her with fear.

She rushed inside and grabbed her keys, not caring that she was wearing shorts and an old T-shirt with dirt on her knees. She didn't even stop to put on a pair of shoes, only realising her feet were bare only when she pulled up at the gate of Fallon and Jon's property.

She was right; the ambulance was parked outside their big shed. She jumped out of the car, slammed the door, and ran across the dirt to the shed just as Fallon came out of the house carrying young Ryan.

'Oh my God,' Alice said, 'I'm so pleased to see you. Are you all right? Is Jon okay?'

'Yes, he is.'

'Please tell me that Billy and Beau are all right, too?' Alice started to cry, tears streaming down her face. She put her hand up to her face. Fallon came over and put one arm around her shoulder.

'Billy and Beau are fine. It's Noreen. She got caught in the cattle crush and has a broken leg. We weren't sure about internal injuries. That's why the ambulance was in such a hurry. They've decided not to move her until the RFDS arrives The helicopter's on the way.'

'Oh my God, I was so worried.'

'You were worried it was Billy, weren't you?'

'I was. I did the wrong thing. Oh, Fallon, I made a mistake. A huge mistake. I told him I didn't want to see him anymore.'

'And you didn't mean it, obviously.'

'No, I didn't mean it. When I thought it could have been him, I knew. I've been so stupid.'

'Well, you'd better sort it out because he's been grumbling around here like a bear with a sore head since Wednesday afternoon. Even Beau got sick of him and came up and had dinner with us last night. Billy's in love with you, Alice.'

Her eyes widened. 'You really think so?'

'I do, but that's something you have to sort out between yourselves. Okay?'

'I will,' she said quietly. 'Where is he now?'

'He's with Beau, back at their place. Beau got upset when he heard the ambulance—it brought a lot of his sad memories back. I made them a hot drink, and they went home. They've not long been gone. It brought tears to my eyes. Billy had his arm around Beau, and Beau wouldn't let him go. He's a beautiful young man, and I think he's just realising how much Billy loves him.'

'Thank you. I hope that poor young woman is all right. She's the wife of the chef at the hotel, isn't she?'

'Yes, that's the one. Robbo is on his way out now.'

'Okay, now I know you guys are all okay, and there's nothing I can do, I'll go back to my place. Unless I can help?'

'No, it's fine.'

'Okay. Please don't tell Billy I was here.'

'Are you sure, Alice?'

'Yes, I've got a lot of thinking to do.'

***

Billy sat on the front porch of the old house, staring out over the paddocks. It had taken a good hour to settle Beau, and he had gone to bed without any dinner. He cried himself to sleep after having a shower, and Billy sat beside him, his hand on his shoulder, until the young boy drifted off.

As Billy gazed down at him, he could see so much of his sister in Beau's features and a deep sadness lodged in his chest. He thought about moving away, but he knew it would be cruel. It wasn't the right thing for young Beau.

He was settled here, in school, and had made good friends. Billy knew he had as much work as he needed while he wanted it—all he didn't have was Alice.

But he was going to do something about that. If Beau went to school tomorrow, he would go and see her. Beau was his priority at the moment; he had to put his feelings aside.

He patted his pocket for a cigarette, remembering again that he had given up smoking. In times of stress, his hand still automatically went there, looking for comfort. He hadn't had a beer tonight either because he wanted to stay awake in case Beau needed him during the night. They had a good heart-to-heart, and Beau had let out a lot of grief he'd been holding inside. It was the most Billy had ever seen him cry.

Billy stood and stretched, his eyes narrowing as he saw the headlights of a car coming up his driveway. His heart started pounding hard as the car moved closer, and he realised it was Alice's small red sedan.

'What's wrong now?' he wondered. The helicopter had gone over two hours ago, and he hoped that Noreen would be okay.

He waited at the top of the steps as Alice got out of the car and walked across to him. She stood at the bottom and looked up at him, and there was enough light for him to see her expression. He wasn't sure who moved first, but they met in the middle, and he put his arms around her, burying his face in her shoulder.

'This is where I have to be.' Her breath

warmed his skin as she spoke quietly. 'This is where I want to be.'

'Where, Alice? Tell me.' Billy lifted his head, and her breath hitched as she reached out and touched his face.

'With you. Wherever you are.' Her voice was soft as his eyes held hers.

'And I want to be with you, too. Wherever you are, I can leave the land. I can go back to an office job if that helps you. We don't have to work in the country. Unless you want to stay?'

'I love my job, and I love living in this town. I was wrong, Billy. I want you to do what you love.'

'What I love? I love you, Alice.'

***

Joy, like Alice had never known, flooded through her. She lifted her arms around his neck and pulled Billy's head closer to hers.

'Kiss me.' She pressed her lips against his mouth. 'Kiss me. Please, kiss me.' Warm lips moved against hers, and she remembered the first time he had kissed her the night after they'd had dinner in the hotel. 'Kiss me as if you can't bear to let me go.' An unbelievable feeling ran through her as Billy's hold tightened, and she

261

closed her eyes. As his lips claimed hers, a chuckle came from the porch above them.

Alice pulled back and looked up into Beau's smiling face.

'About bloody time,' he said.

CHAPTER 34
The Augathella Masquerade Ball

Gladys Tingle stood on the raised stage next to a huge flower arrangement that graced the stage. Chloe and Rosie had donated the floral arrangements for the night, and even though the ball was being held on their premises, they had gone above and beyond. Gladys had never seen flowers like it in her whole life. Not even in Brisbane.

The tables for eight were beautifully decorated, and she was pleased to see the little pink bells she had crocheted were sitting in the middle of each table. Tickets had been sold far and wide, and according to Fallon, who'd supervised the online ticket sales, guests had come from as far away as Longreach and Roma. It was certainly going to be an excellent fundraiser.

Gladys nodded. She could see this ball becoming an annual event on the Augathella calendar, which pleased her as she would miss their weekly meetings in the tea rooms.

Lightness filled her heart as she looked

around at the couples dancing on the floor below the stage. Even the band was playing decent music, none of that modern stuff. She closed her eyes and let the music take her back to her teenage years when she met Harry at Cloudland in Brisbane. She had gone from Augathella to Brisbane to stay with her cousin, and that had been her introduction to music and dancing. She'd loved it ever since. She had fallen in love that night, and eventually, her Harry had come home to Augathella with her.

They had had a wonderful life, and she'd loved him dearly. He'd been a fine husband, but sadly, they'd only been blessed with one child. Tilly's father worked in a mine up near Mt Isa; she hadn't seen him for ten years but was thankful for the Christmas and birthday cards she received.

Gladys knew she had turned into a bitter old woman as she'd aged, but over the past few months, spending time with her granddaughter, Tilly, and the younger women in town and her friend, Beryl, she'd felt her heart lighten.

Nowadays, she thought before she spoke. She had said some nasty things and been rude to a lot of people over the years, but now it was time to make amends. She loved living in Augathella and she was enjoying her time in the aged care facility. It was time for her to start living another happy life.

She opened her eyes and smoothed down the skirt of her shantung ball dress. Tilly had taken her shopping in Longreach a few months back, and Gladys had laughed when Tilly held up the ball dress and said, 'This will look beautiful on you, Nana.'

'Don't be silly. I don't need to wear a ball dress,' Gladys replied.

'You do,' Tilly insisted. 'And I've made you a mask to match it. I saw this dress up here last time I was here, and I asked them to put it away. I knew it would fit you.'

'You're a good girl, love. But I can't afford it.'

But Tilly had insisted. 'It's your Christmas present from me.'

Now Gladys looked down at her shantung dress as the purple and pink reflected in the spinning light above the dance floor. She smiled; life had been happier since Tilly had come home, and Jeremy, her young man, was a delight.

Tilly looked stunning in her royal blue

ballgown, and Jeremy's bow tie was the same shade of blue.

Everyone had excelled themselves tonight. The men wore dinner suits or good trousers and dress shirts with bow ties, and every woman was in a ball dress. Watching the dancing was like watching a rippling rainbow; even the children were dressed up.

In the adjacent room, there was a second, smaller dance floor for the children, and when the music volume decreased in the main ballroom, she could hear the laughter and squeals as the children enjoyed the ball as much as the adults.

Even the children wore masks, and there was much hilarity as koalas greeted cockatoos and rosellas played with echidnas. The masks of the adults were much more Venetian, with some faces totally covered except for the eyes.

Callie, Sophie, and Alice had excelled themselves. Even Gladys had to admit that. She reached up and gently touched the beaded purple mask that covered two-thirds of her face. Her eyes were all she needed tonight, and she was having great fun standing up in the corner of the stage behind the flower arrangement, trying to figure out who was who beneath the colourful masks.

It wasn't too hard. She could pick the colour of the men's hair and whether the women were pregnant or not. Callie and Braden were impossible to miss, even though they had huge masks that covered their entire faces. Matching bronze and gold masks—they were very spectacular, she thought, but she tried not to be uncharitable. Callie had made lovely masks for *everyone*, not just her own.

Callie was easy to spot because of her pregnant stomach. The others were easy to pick, too—Amelia Riley, because of her pregnant stomach and dark hair, and her husband, Ben, because he was one of the few men singing along in full voice with the music. She was surprised that someone who sang country and western with Matt Hunter would know the words to these old songs. At the moment, he was crooning, *'It's Amore',* and he sounded just like Frank Sinatra.

Memories hugged Gladys. That was her old life of many, many years ago, and she and Harry had made a good life in Augathella.

Now that she was in her twilight years—the last time she said that Tilly had tapped her on the wrist and said, 'Nana, you're not in your twilight years yet.'

'Sweetheart, I live in an aged care facility,' she said.

Tilly hugged her and said, 'Well, it's still not your twilight years.'

A couple crossed in front of the stage, and it took her a few minutes to figure out who they were. Then she realised it was Fallon and Jon Ingram. Fallon was pregnant, but her dress concealed her stomach. Their masks were red and blue.

Sophie and Kent Mason twirled across the floor, showing off their dance skills. Gladys was sure they would win the prize for the best mask. Sophie had excelled herself with the ones they wore.

Braden and Callie Cartright danced by sedately because Braden could barely get his arms around his wife; she was so big with her pregnancy.

Goodness, she thought, there was going to be a need for an extension to the primary school with all these pregnant women. Amelia and Ben Foley danced past the bottom of the stage, and Amelia looked up and smiled at her. She was the sweetest young woman.

Next in the dance line were Laura and Dr Harry. Gladys had a soft spot for Dr Harry as he shared her late husband's name. He had always been very kind to her, and Laura, even though she'd been prickly when she'd first come to town, was a lovely person. Laura always called into Gladys' room to say hello when she was at the facility.

Gladys pursed her lips as Beryl swept past in the arms of Ward Whelan, the new butcher in town.

Silly woman; she was old to be dancing.

But Gladys looked down longingly as Beryl smiled. Maybe she wasn't too old to dance.

The tempo of the music changed to one of those modern songs that Gladys didn't know. Many of the dancing couples headed to their table for a rest, but Bec and Matt Hunter moved to the middle of the dance floor. They started doing some sort of rock'n roll dance in the middle of the floor, and two local couples stood back, clapping at them.

Kimberley Calthorpe, who was also pregnant, clapped her hands and laughed as Matt lifted Bec high in the air. Jenna and Josh Foley stood beside them, and Gladys could hear Jenna's loud laughter over the music.

On the other side of the room were those she still called the newcomers to town, and even though they were newcomers, they'd done an amazing job in the last eighteen months since Chloe and her New Life crew had come to town.

But the couple that made her heart sing were Billy Burke and Alice Templeton. Seeing them in each other's arms filled her with happiness. They'd been inseparable over the last two weeks, and last she'd heard—Gladys folded her arms and nodded—Alice was moving in with Billy and young Beau.

Ward Whelan ran lightly up the stairs to the stage and held out his hand. 'Come on, Gladys Tingle. You can't be a wallflower. I think this dance is mine.'

Fancy a young man wanting to dance with an old lady like her.

Gladys smiled as she took his hand and joined her friends on the dance floor. It was a long time since she'd rock and rolled with Harry, but she'd give it a go.

Soon, Jenna and Kiblerley were clapping them. Ward certainly knew his moves, and

Gladys dug deep for the energy to keep up with him. They soon had an audience, and the look on Tilly's face made Gladys' night.

'There's no doubt,' she said to Ward as he escorted her back to her table when the band took a break, 'The Augathella Masquerade Ball ball is a huge success.'

Just after ten o'clock, Callie touched Braden's hand. 'I've had it, love. I cannot dance another step, even though I'm loving every moment of it.'

Braden put his arm around her and escorted her over to a soft lounge near the bar. 'You sit here, and I'll get you a lemonade.'

'Thank you.' Callie eased her feet out of her flat shoes and looked at them with a smile. Shoes she'd bought in Brisbane before she'd met Braden and their boys. Shoes that had almost been ruined in the deluge of water that had run down the irrigation channel the day Braden had rescued her and her luggage. Her first day in Augathella and the day that she first laid her eyes on Braden Cartwright. Callie smiled as Petie crept in from the children's ballroom.

'Mummy, can I have a little bit more money, please?' he asked

'Some more money? What do you want that for, sweetheart?'

'There's a girl here from school, and I asked her if she'd like a drink, and she said she would.'

'Of course, sweetheart, that's very kind of you.' Callie reached the small reticule that was sewn on the side of her ball dress. Her stomach was so big that the small purse had slipped around, and she couldn't reach it.

'Can you reach it for me, Petie?' She pointed to the little velvet purse. 'Take a couple of dollars. Will that be enough?'

'That will. Thanks, Mummy. Love you.'

Callie smiled as she watched him run back to the other room. Rory and Nigel were feeling very grown-up tonight, and they looked it when they both put their suits on. Along with Beau Burke, she'd had taken them to the op shop together in Charleville a few weeks ago and managed to find suits that fitted the three of them. She knew that Rory had his eye on one of the girls in Year Six, and she smiled as they danced past the doorway half an hour ago.

Callie sat back and put her hands on her stomach. She closed her eyes and let the love in the ballroom surround her—the love for her man, the love for all their children, and the love of their friends and family, and all the joyous people in this room tonight.

She sent a quiet prayer up to Julia, Rory, Nigel, and Petie's mother. 'I'll look after them for you, Julia, until I take my last breath.'

Braden came back with her lemonade and put his arm around her. 'Okay, sweetheart?'

'More than okay,' Callie whispered. 'I love this community, and I will never regret the day I came to Augathella.

'And Augathella loves you, just as we all do.

Callie lifted her face for her husband's kiss.

She lived in a wonderful community, and she knew she would never live anywhere else.

THE END

OTHER PRINT BOOKS FROM ANNIE

Available on Annie's store and Amazon:
https://annieseatonstore.ecwid.com/

New Series: The Daughters of The Darling
1: From Across the Sea
2. Over the River (November 2024)
Other books
Bowen River (Dec 2024)
Whitsunday Dawn
Undara
Osprey Reef
East of Alice
Porter Sisters Series
Kakadu Sunset
Daintree
Diamond Sky
Hidden Valley
Larapinta
Kakadu Dawn
Pentecost Island Series
Pippa
Eliza
Nell
Tamsin

Evie

Cherry

Odessa

Sienna

Tess

Isla

Also available in three boxed sets

Books 1-3

Books 4-6

Books 7-10

The Augathella Girls Series

Outback Roads

Outback Sky

Outback Escape

Outback Wind

Outback Dawn

Outback Moonlight

Outback Dust

Outback Hope

Augathella Short and Sweet Series

An Augathella Surprise

An Augathella Baby

An Augathella Spring

An Augathella Christmas

Love Across Time Series
Come Back to Me
Follow Me
Finding Home
The Threads that Bind
Love Across Time 1-4 Boxed Set
Bindarra Creek
Worth the Wait
Full Circle
Secrets of River Cottage
A Clever Christmas
A Bindarra Creek Duo
A Place to Belong
Four Seasons Short and Sweet
Ten Days in Paradise
Follow the Sun
Others
Deadly Secrets
Adventures in Time
Silver Valley Witch
The Emerald Necklace
Christmas with the Boss
Her Christmas Star
An Aussie Christmas Duo (two Christmas novellas)

ABOUT THE AUTHOR

Annie lives in Australia, on the beautiful north coast of New South Wales. She sits in her writing chair and looks out over the tranquil Pacific Ocean.

She writes contemporary romance and loves telling stories that always have a happily ever after. She lives with her very own hero of many years and they share their home with Toby, the naughtiest dog in the universe, and Barney, the ragdoll puss, who hides when the four grandchildren come to visit.

Stay up to date with her latest releases at her website: http://www.annieseaton.net

AWARDS

2023: Winner of the long contemporary RUBY award for Larapinta

Finalist for the NZ KORU Award 2018 and 2020.

Winner ...Best Established Author of the Year 2017 AUSROM

Longlisted for the Sisters in Crime Davitt Awards 2016, 2017, 2018, 2019

Finalist in Book of the Year, Long Romance, RWA Ruby Awards 2016 Kakadu Sunset

Winner ...Best Established Author of the Year 2015 AUSROM

Winner ...Author of the Year 2014 AUSROM

Best Established Author, Ausrom Readers' Choice   2017

Book of the Year

9 781923 048614